MW01148192

Pimping Ain't Easy:

But somebody's gotta do it

A Novel

By

Mickey Royal

Copyright

Library of Congress Cataloging-in-Publication Data is available upon request.

Manufactured in the United States of America
Cover Model: Cheyanne Foxx

Published by:
Sharif Media
6709 La Tijera blvd
#567
La, Ca 90045

Dedication

This book is dedicated to the lives of Malcolm X and Maya Angelou.

Malcolm X- Minister, author, civil rights activist and former self-admitted pimp.

Maya Angelou- Poet, civil rights activist, author and former self-admitted prostitute.

Warning

This book is written in a style called Faction (Fact/Fiction). Certain facts have been omitted and events have been slightly altered in order to keep innocent people from being murdered.

Any killings discussed have to have already been solved or be public or street knowledge because there is no statute of limitations on murder. I have never and will never say or write anything that will incriminate myself or any of my friends, relatives or even enemies.

Table of Contents

Mickey Royal

To my Readers

I appreciate your patronage as well as your loyalty to my books. You incarcerated readers in particular have been my inspiration. Furthermore, I was so tired of pseudo intellectuals writing books about a lifestyle they've never lived, but insisting on passing themselves off as experts and expecting us to be too stupid to know the difference. Thank you for knowing the difference.

Respectfully Yours,

Mickey Royal

Mickey Royal age one. Surrounded by girls older than himself. Not much has changed since.

Mickey Royal age 13. The first night he made over 1,000 selling crack and weed on the block, about that life early.

Jay Supreme (left) Mickey Royal (right) at age 13.
Note; Mickey Royal's gold chain, gold watch and
beeper, truly about that life.

Mickey Royal at age 17 as an F.O.I. from Muhammad's Mosque #27. He was also under the tutelage of B.K.F Kenpo legend Steve Muhammad. At age 17 Martial Arts and Islam were his main focusses. He was no longer in the life.

Mickey Royal(left), Jay Supreme(right) with matching green Cadillac's in their early 20's. About that life once again.

Jay Supreme(left) and Mickey Royal(right) with matching silver Cadillacs in their early 30's. Jay Supreme went on to produce such hits as "This is How we do it" by Montel Jordan and "Back in the Day" by Ahmad and "Throw your Hands up" by LV among others. Mickey Royal went on to direct over 100 adult films.

Mickey Royal

Chapter 1

Saturday, March 15th

Solidifying a stance on the street is a never-ending journey. For the concrete and brick that blankets the asphalt jungle are as solid as coffin nails, the streets are like Desert sands that change formation with the wind. A mountain today can be a valley tomorrow. It's a delicate balance of power which changes by the hour. In an instant, your life can change permanently.

Like tonight, as my Cadillac slowly cruises through Hollywood my eyes are open, the air is thick and the vibe is electric. Hollywood has a heartbeat all its own. Separate from Los Angeles. Hollywood has a code.

I pulled up at my main lady Cheyanne Foxx's spot on Fountain and Seward. She had a two-bedroom, two bath condo in a gated building.

Her sister had come to stay with her recently. Her boyfriend kicked her out and she had nowhere to go. I sat outside downstairs in the car for 10 minutes before I went up. Just tired, and I've read this story before. I usually wouldn't even consider meeting her except for the fact that Cheyanne Foxx had begged me to come pick her up.

I have a rule of not dealing with recent kick outs. Too much training involved. A recent kick out is just looking for a quick fix to a long-term problem. They're more trouble than they're worth. Despite what they say as soon as boyfriend calls they're going to disappear. Knowing all of this, and yet;

"Hey Mickey, this is Coffee. Turn around and let him see you" said Cheyanne as she was displaying her like a model on the runway.

Coffee turned two circles slowly. She was 22 years old and drop dead gorgeous. I knew at that moment I would never let her go. The moment we locked eyes she belonged to me. I didn't ask Cheyanne why she couldn't live with her temporarily, but I was certain I'd eventually find out. I hung out there with them for about 10 to 15 minutes before Coffee and I left.

I walked her to the car. She was surprised I had opened the door for her. From her pause and her forced smile, I knew from there she had preconceived notions of who I was and what I was about.

16

"I'm doing a thesis on the life and I'd like to study you." She opened with. I laughed then it all made sense. Normally I'd never agree to such incriminating foolishness, but I must admit I was intriguingly flattered.

As we drove down Santa Monica Blvd towards La Brea avenue she began to explain her project. The more she spoke it began to sound more like I was an animal being studied by National Geographic. Still, I was interested. I had no expression on my face. I let her talk herself nervous until we reached the point of an uncomfortable silence.

We pulled up at Pinks hot dog stand and I looked into her beautiful sleepy eyes and said,

"Hungry?"

She actually pulled out her note pad and began to write. This was weird.

"I wish to ride with you and observe and report your daily/nightly activities," she explained.

She was young and innocent, not at all from the life. In the upside, backwards life called The Pimp Game this made perfect sense. As we walked to the front window to place our orders she pulled out that note pad yet again to write down what I ordered.

"May I have one turkey dog with mustard, chili, and grilled mushrooms."

I have no idea what she scribbled in that book of hers but her hand was moving.

"Coffee, what would you like?"

"What do you recommend?"

She didn't look like much of an eater, so I ordered her a Chicago Dog with onion rings and a Key Lime-flavored soda. We sat on the back patio, split the onion rings and soda between the two of us.

"Cheyanne knew better than to tell me upfront what this was about."

"Why do you say that?" Coffee asked.

"Because I would have never agreed to it. I'm, only doing this because she asked me to. I live in a secret society. We operate in the shadows of inequity. Hidden in plain sight by day."

As we sat and ate I was analyzing her body language. Looking for a hint of an ulterior motive. I trusted Cheyanne but I didn't quite trust Miss Coffee as of yet. So, I kept the conversation light until I did, or if I'd ever.

"What school do you attend?"

"USC. I'm a psychology major. This is for my behavioral science class. Just go about your daily routine as if I'm not here. I will observe and report only."

"Everything has a price sweetheart," I said to Coffee with a wry evil grin, eyebrow raised with sinister curiosity.

"Whatever you say," she replied.

Then she continued by saying,

"Cheyanne said I could stay the week with you. I have this week off, you know Spring Break. My assignment is due next Monday. Must be 1,500 words or more."

As we sat there and ate I noticed the police had pulled up. I told her to pack it up. She didn't hesitate. Coffee gathered up what was left of our meal and we headed for the car. I wasn't wanted nor did I have any warrants but Mickey Royal doesn't dine with swine.

"Let's go Coffee, it's starting to stink over here," I said loud enough for the pigs to hear me.

"Cheyanne was telling me about some boyfriend of yours."

"Yeah, we got into it and he kicked me out. I'm going by tomorrow to get my things."

"Do you require my assistance? Not because I actually care. Just wanted to know if I had to squeeze domestic activities into my schedule."

"I don't know, I have to call him first and set up a time."

As we were driving back towards my spot I was having second thoughts about this project of hers. Then the phone rang, and it was Sweet Pea checking in;

"Daddy I'm leaving the club headed to the after-hours."

"Which one"

"Downtown"

"How we looking?"

"Four and some change, so far"

"Pick it up and stay down"

"Always daddy"

I answered the phone on speaker knowing shed get a kick out of the language. Her little pencil was moving. We pulled up at my spot in the marina.

"We're here, Coffee."

20

"This is where you live?" She asked.

"I work, I don't live anywhere. This is one of the spots I store clothing if that's what you're asking."

"I mean where do you sleep?"

"I don't." I continued because I could see the perplexed look on her face.

"I go to bed wherever I happened to be when I get sleepy. So, you and Cheyanne are sisters? She never mentioned you."

"We're not really sisters. Her sister and I are best friends, so she always calls me her sister."

"Remember when I said everything comes with a price?" I could see fear in her eyes for the first time.

"Yes." She replied, voice cracking trying not to show any fear, any weakness." I escorted her to the bedroom.

"Take off your clothes," I commanded.

Coffee did just as I ordered without hesitation. I could tell she was afraid of me. I was comfortable with this fear, accustomed to it. I've seen it, caused it in the eyes of many men and women. She stripped down to her panties and bra.

"Must I repeat myself?" she took a deep breath, rolled her eyes and continued.

Her hands were trembling as she could visibly see I was taking sheer pleasure in this display.

Her trembling hands made it difficult for her to grasp the clasp of her bra.

"Here, let me help you."

I ripped her bra completely from her body in one swooping motion with my left hand. I spent her around, leaning her forward across the bed. I ripped off her panties with my right hand. She was bent over in front of me, scare to death. I went to my guest closet where I kept female clothing for special overnight guests. Coffee was getting far too familiar with me, too comfortable for my comfort.

No woman is to ever be that relaxed in my company except my wives and she isn't one of them. She was perched in my bed on all fours awaiting my next command. I could see she was expecting the inevitable rape as an initiation. A declaration of trust if you will. As she arched her back I rubbed her ass very gently then threw her a curve ball.

"Put this on, see if it fits you." I ordered.

She nor anyone else should ever be able to anticipate a pimp's next move. Every move I make, every word I speak is to establish and or maintain

power in some way. I could literally hear her exhale
a sign of relief as she turned around to inspect the
outfit I had picked out for her to change into. That's
when I went to retrieve my camera from my closet.

"Pull your skirt up. Push your panties to the side,
more! That's it. Hold."

I began snapping provocative pictures of
her. I posed her with a dildo's and teddy bears. I
made her sign a model release.

"Don't worry sweetheart, no one will ever see these
pictures. They will be deleted following the end of
your project."

"Then why take em?" she asked with a slight bit of
hostility in her voice.

"I've been interviewed before by a reporter from the
Newspaper. He put words in my mouth. He
expressed untruths in his article that showed me in
an improper light. I was betrayed. This way if I'm
humiliated so shall you be."

"I understand," she answered.

"Do you?" I sternly asked as I tossed her the
newspaper article about a Times journalist which
read;

'Murdered in an attempted carjacking.'
She slowly put the paper on the bed. She only had
to read the headline.

There was no need to read further. Our eyes met and I said, "Don't betray my trust Ms. Coffee."

She nodded her head twice slowly as if she fully understood the potential consequences.

"Are you sure you want to do this?"

"I'm sure"

"Okay, then welcome to my world. I'm Mickey Royal. I need not know your real name. No one uses their government names in the life."

"I'm not a neophyte in this area Mr. Royal. I know a little bit about the underworld. And Coffee is actually my birth name."

"Sweetheart make no mistake. This isn't the Underworld, this is The Shadow World. Cloaked by day, camouflaged in plain sight."

I was satisfied with our banter once I saw her mood go from fear to confidence to anxiety. If she's comfortable in my presence and she's not a Royal Family member, then I'm doing something wrong.
As she sat there anticipating my next move, pondering what words, what command would next exit my lips I handed her an outfit more suitable for our destination.

"You look like a size 6. Here put this on." I handed her a black leather skirt with a matching black halter top.

"These are whore clothes," she said as she put them on with enthusiasm.

"Camouflage Coffee, for the type of jungle we're entering. In that pants suit you look like a cop or a social worker."

"Where are you going?"

"To take a shower. Pimps do bathe you know." I grinned, she smiled.

It was important to me for her to see me in all of my glory and yet remain an unsolved mystery.
She watched as I picked out yet another all black outfit. I laid out my lamb skin full-length black trench coat. I also laid out my black leather gloves. I could tell she was interested in the life, not just as a case study. Her body language told more of her story than her words. Just then I excused myself to go shower in private.

"If you would please excuse me," I said humbly as I went into the restroom.

I purposefully left her alone in the room with open closets and drawers. It was done not to necessarily show trust but to show I wasn't too concerned with whatever ulterior motive she might have up her sleeve. A true pimp never trusts period. The newspaper caption still had her spooked. Any further intimidation would be overkill.

Besides this was a favor for Cheyanne Foxx, my closest ally. I kept that in mind while dealing with Coffee. A friend of a friend makes her a friend. But still I am who and what I am and my vampiric fangs are out, dripping with poisonous venom commonly known as Game, to the outsiders. But true pimps refer to it as the Izm.

Turning Coffee out would pose no challenge to me at all. She'd be good for 1,500 a day easy. That's 10,500 a week. That's 546,000 a year. These figures calculated in my head in seconds the moment Coffee looked into my eyes and asked

"How do I look? Am I ready?"

"You look passable." I responded to her while getting dressed.

I was watching her eyes watch me closely, writing in her little memo book.

"Let's go!" I ordered with authority."

"Where are we going?" she asked.

"Understand this is highly irregular and potentially dangerous. You are to walk at least two steps behind me. You don't ask me any questions in public. Do not pull out that memo book and write anything down. Write all you want in the car. Do not make eye contact with anyone male or female. If asked a question look directly into my eyes.

Then I will answer any question asked of you for you. Do not wander off and stay close to me."

As we approached the car, I finished our little orientation with;

"Oh, and ride in the back seat." I opened the door for her in classic pimp form.

"In you go darling. First stop, The Tracks." I said like a cab driver flipping on his meter. I could have taken the freeway but I decided to take the streets. First track I hit was Figueroa in South Central.

"This is the first track I ever worked. This is where most LA pimps first got their feet wet. Cross-country pimping or pimping PI (Pimping International) or whatever. The inner-city is where you started. Most pimps, true pimps are self-created. Some pimps were put in place or put on by a bigger boss.
Be it a big-time loan shark, drug dealer, or hustler. But the ones who sustained thru time are the ones who started with the mere basics.
This is where you get your education from the world's greatest teacher... Experience! Coincidentally it's also the most expensive form of education/ It can take all of your money and all of your time before you learn the lesson it intended to teach you. It starts with one man, one woman, and an exit plan. The exit plan is where the complications lie.

To become a seasoned Professional Gentleman of Leisure one must endure a series of trials and tribulations. Every scar on my body has a story to tell. The deepest scars are the ones that aren't visible with the naked eye. They last forever. This life, this game changes you permanently. You will literally feel yourself metamorphosing into another celestial body while feeling your once inner self slip away and eventually die. Once you enter The Pimp Game you'll never be the same."

I wanted to help Coffee but at the same time protect her from the horrors of my world. Coffee was the first woman I had been around in a long time who wasn't from the life. Her naïve nature and juvenile questioning was actually a breath of fresh air. But on the street, in the life you can't afford to forget for one minute who you are, where you are and what it is that you do.

This is an error-free lifestyle where your first mistake can oftentimes be your last. I wanted to make sure I painted a realistic picture of what she saw. At the same time not losing sight of the fact that I have a job to do and a life to live.

"Is this the track?" she asked.

"Naw, not yet. This is the hood. In the hood every street looks like a track after 9pm."

Coffee was leaning forward in the backseat. Poised and alert as if she was on an African Safari and I was Abdul her trusted tour guide.

"This is the edge of the first track I ever worked. You'll begin to notice the number of cheap motels and all-night liquor stores."

"Is she a ho?" asked Coffee as she pointed out at a woman walking.

"Sweetheart don't stare and please don't point. Try to relax, and technically no, she's a crackhead who is ho-ing."

"How can you tell?'

"The wide eyes, fast walk with folded arms. She's cold so she's fully dressed. Her price can be from 5 dollars to 150 depending on how strong she's currently 'Jonesing' multiplied by how green or desperate the trick is who pulls up. Each trick, each John is a separate negotiation. No real set prices. They're providing a service not selling a product."

Coffee was immediately fascinated. I gazed up at the rearview mirror and saw her with her mouth wide open with a look of shock. There are distinct differences between hookers, whores, crack whores, prostitutes, escorts, call girls, and adult entertainers. I've worked with all in my lifetime. Each one is different which require a different

approach and management technique. A pimp's
style is based on three main elements:

1. Who he was before he entered the game;
2. What type of women he has in his stable;
3. The activity or opportunities he has in front of
him or potentially to create.

"Coffee, I'll break down the differences later for
you. But for now, just chill and keep your eyes and
ears open. And by all means, try and look relaxed."

As we passed 120th cross the train tracks
under the freeway coming up to Imperial Hwy and
Figueroa Coffee noticed I became more alert.

"Can we pull into 'Jack in the Box' I need to
tinkle." Coffee whispered inner little girl voice.

Maybe she was flirting, or maybe being in the
presence of The Izm has her sliding into character.
It was too early to tell so I didn't process it. I just
made a right into Jack in the Box parking lot.
Coffee was apparently new to hood surroundings.
Businesses in these neighborhoods lock their doors
at 8pm. Only the drive-thru is still open. Instead of
explaining this to her I parked.

"I'll wait for you baby." I said to her in a slow deep
Billy Dee Williams drawl.

She slid out of the backseat walking with her legs
clinched together trying not to urinate on herself at

the same time embarrassingly pulling her skirt down which kept rising with each step.

Just as I thought, Coffee came back to the car legs clinched.

"That asshole said lobby closed. Lobby closed? Bastard!"

"Here, just squat by the car."

Coffee froze for the longest 5 seconds in the history of the annals of time as she processed having to actually urinate on the street in public. I could see it was totally out of her character as she stepped momentarily out of character and squatted. I made sure to keep constant eye contact during this most embarrassing moment for her.

I mentioned to her about paying a price. She's already changing right before her very own eyes but doesn't realize it. If you dance with the Devil one time or all night it doesn't matter. The Devil never changes the song nor do you change the Devil. The Devil changes you.

Her walk, her persona, what she is willing or not willing to do were slowly being compromised. And we haven't even started. No matter how you sneak up on a mirror it always looks you right in the eyes.

Coffee re-entered the backseat with a stench of urine that I made a point to verbally point out, then excuse. Watching her transform before her very own eyes without effort from myself, was not my intent. The goal is to baptize Coffee in the sinful waters of the game without her getting wet. At this moment, I didn't see how that was possible.

"He could have let me in."

"You okay?"

"Yeah I'm okay."

"Let's roll."

As we crossed the light I began to point out what she was seeing;

"To your right in the green is a prostitute. The chick in the red skirt is a ho with a Chili Pimp. A Chili Pimp thinks he's a pimp but he's no more than just a boyfriend with a girlfriend who's selling pussy. He sits close to her at all times basically scaring away would-be tricks and clients without even being aware of the fact. He's learning on the job. He can't teach her anything because he knows less than her. That's the duo who lives from motel to motel.
    She's too jealous and self-absorbed to share him with other ho's. This causes him to never grow as a pimp. He finds himself trapped in the life without growth, development, or prosperity. He's too jealous and self-absorbed to share her with paying customers. She never gets to develop customers into regular clients, because he can't bare the thought of her sleeping with other men. They exist in a sick detrimental co-dependent relationship motivated only by day to day survival."

We continued our journey north on Figueroa to 108th street where we were stopped at the light. I pointed out the pink and white apartment building where the famous rapper Big Lurch got high on PCP and ate his girlfriend to death, chewed and swallowed. Her mouth dropped open in disbelief. I told her to google it on her laptop when we get back to the marina spot.

This was a basic introduction as I, her tour guide drove slowly down these South LA streets. I pointed out various infamous locations like the motel where (GOOGLE AND CHECK FACTS) Sam Cooke was murdered by an Asian hooker. While speaking and labeling these places and people both famous and infamous, I made sure to announce to her which gang neighborhoods we were in.

"We just drove through Denver Lane Blood Gang territory. Once we cross this light the territory belongs to the Hoover Crips."

Some of the gangstas try their hand at Gorilla Pimping but end up petty extortionists. The local gangbangers are the Chili Pimps worst enemy. Since the Chili Pimp never develops his game to becoming a true pimp and later pimping P.I. status he doesn't possess urban diplomacy. His skills of navigation are minimal at best. Thus, he and his one-woman show are forced to move often.

In my Cady, suited in typical pimp fashion with Curtis Mayfield's song 'He's A Fly Guy' playing my mood was interrupted by a phone call. I put the phone on speaker without looking down at the Caller ID as usual.

"Hey you!?" it was Sweet Pea.

Sweet Pea was a sweet only in name. She started with me at 23. Now at age 30 she was a seasoned pro. But being 5'3" and having flawless youthful skin the name still fits and works to her advantage.

Sweet Pea knows never to mention me by name over the telephone. She's also smart enough to know no to reference specifics. We have codes, a secret language if you will. It's not paranoia, it's precaution.

"Yes" I responded.

One word and or short answers are too alert her I'm in mixed company. Mixed company meaning a non-Royal Family member.

"We good!" said Sweet Pea meaning she went over 1,000 dollars today.

"Real good?" I asked Meaning we are over 2,000 today.

"No, pretty good." Meaning 1500 or close to it.
"Kay" meaning I'm okay with the results.

"Copy, out." Copy meant she got the message and Out meant she's officially off the clock.

"Who was that? Was she a prostitute? What did all of that mean?"

"Coffee please save your questions till the end of the lesson" I responded sarcastically.

"Mickey, may I ask you a question?"

"You just did."

I answered swiftly adding just a little deeper base to my eloquent articulate style of speech. Whatever her real question was she wisely chose not to ask it.

"Look Coffee to the left, those are prostitutes from the same stable."

"Wow, how can you tell?"

"Their outfits are styled similar meaning they were selected by the same person possibly at the same time. Notice their positions. One lady near the light pole, two strategically placed on a four-corner stance so no one can be approached from behind. There will be no surprised tricks or undercover cops pulling up without being seen first. They may already have a room or two rented out at the motel they're in front of. She tells the trick he has to pay for the room which is $65.00. The trick usually doesn't want a paper trail so she will walk the 65 dollars over to the window and pocket it. Some motel operators work in unison with the ladies of leisure. The lady may give the proprietor a 20 dollar fee per trick. If so, then the proprietor acts as a lookout. Copying license numbers for extra security or even calling the rooms themselves if police pull into the parking lot."

All of this information at once was a lot for Coffee to digest. As much as she attempted to hide the fact that she was steady writing in that memo book of hers I equally pretended not to notice.

"Are you hungry, thirsty?"

"No sir, I'm fine, well I'm a little hungry."

"Okay, we'll stop and get something in a few."

"When do I get to meet some of your ho's? How many do you have?"

"First of all, I don't have ho's. If you're asking about my wives I must ask that you respectfully refer to them as Ladies of Leisure or wives if you must reference them at all."

I didn't even acknowledge her second question. It was a futile attempt at counting my money. As if I'd fall for that one, I just smiled. Oftentimes people from the university life assume people from the streets are luckily stupid. I didn't bother to waste my time alerting her that the second question insulted my intelligence. People from her world usually can't conceive of people from my world as intelligent in the first place. Therefore, making any commentary from me moot at best. I wanted to just cruise, get something to eat and beguile Coffee with tales from the Darkside so to speak. But things most of the time do not go as planned when it comes to the game. That's why you must always be alert. You must anticipate the next move before obvious signs. By then it's too late to benefit effectively. You'll find yourself a day late and a dollar short. Or simply playing catch up.

"Notice the number of motels and dead-end streets? Some tricks prefer the excitement of dating a prostitute in their car. They park at the end of these dead-end streets. The thrill of doing something naughty and coming dangerously close to getting caught seems to appeal to some."

I pointed out how heads were moving up and down in a lot of the cars parked on the adjacent side streets. Some of the cars were actually rocking side to side. Coffee seemed to be hanging on my every word. I must admit she was good company but I still didn't trust her.

Which came first, the chicken or the egg? The eternal question. I don't know if the motels were built first then Figueroa became a track or if Figueroa was a track then motels were built every 300 feet.

I asked my mentor which came first. He said he came to LA from Memphis, TN in 1962 and it was already a track. This is the longest track I've ever seen and I've been on many tracks nationally and worldwide. It goes from 140th street to King Blvd. (40th street). It stops right at the sports arena. The USC college campus is directly on the other side.

"Do you notice how slow the cars are going in the right lane?"

"Yea, why is that?"

"They're tricks and or just sight-seers, look-e-loos. This is a well-known meat market."

As we approached the end of the track I decided to call it a night. I had conducted most of my daily business before I got to Cheyanne's place.

"What time are you going to pick up your stuff?" I asked Coffee.

Reminding her that she has her own world she lives in and that she's merely a visitor in mines. I wanted to protect her as much as I could. Shielding her away from the real and still give her a realistic picture. But still, my vampiric fangs were dripping at the sight of such an exposed and naive neck. We headed back to the marina.

"I'm hungry!" shouted Coffee.

"Okay, okay, what are you in the mood for?"

"Whatever."

"I have food at the pad, you cook?"

Coffee looked disappointed. It was starting to feel like a date and I didn't want that vibe with her. Besides, she's a family member/friend of my best friend Cheyanne Foxx. I didn't want to disrespectfully cross lines.

"Cook? Are you gonna cook?"

"Coffee baby I'm not the hungry one. Where are you staying? I mean which hotel?"

I knew good and well she had nowhere to go. This was my way of reminding her to remind herself who's doing whom the favor here. As soon as we walked in Coffee headed straight to the kitchen. I went and turned on some jazz, poured myself a glass of sherry and sat on the couch. Coffee had already gone in my kitchen without permission and pulled out some leftover roast duck I had the night before.

Coffee was starting to become comfortable in my presence. As much as I was holding back it was little to no avail. The Izm was seeping through me, flowing, swimming inside of her head patiently waiting to absorb her soul. I could hear her opening and closing the refrigerator door numerous times. I could hear the beeping of the microwave as she pressed button after button trying to reheat my dinner from last night. She was making herself at home as I predicted.

I kept telling myself this is a square 22 year old college girl, leave her alone. But still.....

"This turkey is greasy"

"That's because it's duck sweetheart" I replied still not looking back.

"Oh, you made this?"

"No actually Cheyanne was over two nights ago. She made it. She cooks like a chef."

"I know. She used to own a restaurant."

When Coffee said that Cheyanne used to own a restaurant I pretended like I already knew. Even though it was the first id heard of it. I was surprised Cheyanne never mentioned it. But in all fairness, there's plenty she doesn't know about me either. She sat and ate in the kitchen at the bar.

"How long have you known Cheyanne?"

She really wants to know how close we are and the true nature of our relationship. This I could tell by the way she sat up, inhaled right before asking then asked as she exhaled. Reading her body language was as if a professor at MIT was in a 3rd grade general ed classroom. All too easy. She posed no challenge to me at all. The only challenge that was ever present was my intention vs. my true nature.

"I've known Cheyanne forever and a day. In this life as well as the last."

That was a polite way of saying none of your business. I get in your head, you don't get in mine.

"Funny, she's never mentioned you."

Now she's trying to get dialogue started. I had to keep in mind that she's only 22. She hasn't matured enough to learn that insults are not conversation starters. This was her primitively juvenile attempt to lure me into a detailed conversation. To 'open up' so to speak.

As the premiere master/author of the pimp game I found it rude and presumptuous. If you're going to poke a lion with a stick, make sure the gate is locked. The main elements of the Izm are power and control.

Long before this lady was even born I had mastered both. The base for both are inner power and self-control. In my youth, I was a powerful serpent. At the level I am now, I'm a sinister fire breathing dragon. Comfortable in my skin and familiar with my abilities.

"She's never mentioned you either. Maybe she wanted to keep her left life and her right life separated. Maybe she never intended for us to meet." I replied insinuating that I represent the forbidden fruit.

She got up from the bar leaving her plate and came over to the couch, plopping so close to me our thighs touched.

"And why do you think that is? I'm a big girl"

"Are you finished eating? If so, please clean up behind yourself."

There was embarrassment in her eyes as her expression turned somber.

"Oh, my bad."

She walked over to do as I instructed. While her back was turned I walked into the bedroom. She said something to me. I assumed she asked a question because her voice got higher at the end of her sentence. But I couldn't make out what she said. Whatever it was it wasn't important to me. She followed me into the room.

"Where are my clothes?" asked Coffee.

"I gave them to the consiglieres to have cleaned. They should be ready in the morning.. Here, sleep in this."
I handed her a clean Versace shirt to sleep in.

"Where do you keep your towels?"
Since I usually have a lady or two or three over on any given night, I had guest rolls prepared.

"Here you go"

Inside the Egyptian cotton towel roll was a shower cap, wash cloth, house shoes, travel size lotion, and toothbrush. For the average individual, this would be an awkward moment. But the only experience I have with awkward moments are causing them.

When the Izm in you is strong there's no such thing as an awkward moment. I didn't want to have sex with her. I could tell her body language and vibe her mind suggested otherwise.

Coffee much like most women who stay over usually spend quite a while in my bathroom. The floor is covered in mink and the décor is eclectically early Victorian. The bedroom is Bohemian/Mediterranean. I spin ladies in a circle and take them around the world. I'm sure she's soaking it all in. Coffee comes out of the bathroom.

"This is the softest towel I've ever used."

"It's Egyptian cotton"

"Where did you but it?"

"Egypt"

"Are you serious?"

"Always" I replied.

She was dressed in my shirt with nothing else but a pair of pink mink house shoes I keep for guests. Coffee was visibly exhausted. I stepped into the shower myself for 5 minutes. When I exited the bathroom, she was snoring. She was passed out diagonally across my black satin sheets.

Coffee was sleeping so hard I couldn't dare wake her to scoot her over. I put on my silk tailormade monogrammed pajamas in classic player fashion. Coffee looked so innocently sexy in my shirt. She had the cutest little feet.

Her vagina was noticeably exposed which left me no choice but to sleep on the living room couch. I wasn't at all sleepy. These are actually my peak hours, but I was bored, so I called it a night. It was hard for me to sleep knowing Coffee was in my room alone. She's a journalism student, naturally inquisitive. I had things I didn't want her rifling through.

Sweet Pea

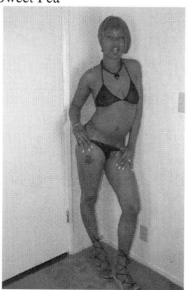

Cheyanne Foxx

Mickey Royal

Chapter 2
Sunday, March 16th

I sleep late and wake up early. I may have
slept five hours, if that. I went into the hallway
restroom to shower up. I didn't wish to disturb
Coffee. I could tell I kept her out way past her bed
time. Even all the while she's determined to
convince me she's a grown up. I decided to trust
Coffee and leave her at the house so I could make
my rounds. I didn't want Coffee's nosy snout and
her memo pad all in my wallet.

I got dressed from clothes in the hallway
and left. When I got to the car I noticed that I had
forgotten and left the house without my phone. I
immediately turned around and headed back to the
elevator from the parking garage.
I was greeted by Coffee as I stepped one foot
through the door.

"Where'd you go?"

"Why?" I responded.

I was taken back by her eager familiarity. Coffee read the lines in my forehead as my widened eyes froze her in her tracks. She seemed to be at a loss for words. She quickly softened her demeanor and smiled in order to get a more accepting expression from me. She recognized immediately that I wasn't her ex-boyfriend nor cut from that tree cloth.

"Oh, because I was worried you had ditched me. I didn't get on your nerves last night, did I?" Coffee said in her Marylin Monroe baby voice.

"No sweetheart, you're good company. I enjoyed having you with me."

Coffee looked so delicious in nothing but my shirt. It was time to turn up the heat.

"Are you coming?"

"I don't have any clean clothes" replied Coffee.

I went to the guest closet.

"What size shoe do you wear?"

"Eight."

I came back with a pair of black leather
thigh high boots.

"Put these on, let's go!"

"I'm not walking outside with a shirt, no panties,
no bra, and boots."

"No, what you're not gonna do is tell me what the
fuck you're not going to do. We can stop this right
now and I can take you wherever it is you came
from. You interrupted a life in progress."

I grabbed the boots in her hand, her memo book and
she darted after me barefoot.

"Hey wait, wait up."

I really didn't want her to come but again I liked the
company. I'm usually alone. At least I had
conversation.

"I know I know in the backseat."

"No Coffee, sit up front. It's daylight."

Right when she thinks she knows the rules I alter
them. Keeping her always on her toes wondering
off balanced and somewhat intrigued.
I've been doing it for so long it's just a
natural instinct at this point.

"Were your bitches on the track last night?"

"I don't associate with bitches but if you're referring to my wives then no, my wives don't walk tracks. Their game has far surpassed any street level activities."

"Then why did you take me out there?"

"Coffee, if you want to teach a child math do you start with arithmetic or calculus?"

Coffee just smiled and nodded in agreement. We pulled up at the Fox Hills mall in Culver City.

"I'm not going in there like this."

She must have read my expression because before I could respond she continued,

"Okay okay alright."

Coffee hopped out of the car and caught up to me so she could walk close enough to confuse my shadow. The stares, the under-the-breath comments I was used to, Coffee wasn't. The more we walked, the closer she walked with me until she had interlocked our arms. She had read my confidence level, power illuminating out of my very pores serving as a beacon of light guiding light no pun intended.

We walked in Victoria's Secret first to pick her out a lace matching panty and bra set that matched my Versace shirt. We walked together

arm-in-arm as we picked out a nice set. We even approached the counter together.
Coffee knew I was going to buy them. I mean she had no purse, no money with her.

"Oh, for me?!"

But more importantly she wanted people in the store to know.

"Go put these on in the dressing room."

We left and went straight to Macy's. I sent her in Macy's alone while I waited at the entrance. As Coffee grew more comfortable she didn't need to walk close to me or with me at all. Teeth adjust to braces and in time the pain goes away. The teeth shift and reshape the entire mouth to conform to the braces without the person wearing them being aware.

"Go hit up the Mac makeup counter and let the sales lady give you a quick makeover and spray on some tester perfume. I'll meet you in the car."

I turned and walked away. I sent her in there dressed that way with no money to test her. I wanted to see if she could finesse an accidental free makeover without a purchase. Coffee smiled, giggled, and flirted just enough without bringing too much attention to herself.
I waited in the car and Coffee came out 10 minutes later made up holding what appeared to be

business cards of some sort. I had no interest in that. Since I didn't specifically ask her to get business cards then I couldn't acknowledge them. That would be equivalent to telling her it's okay to alter my specific instructions.

"Coffee you look so much better, get in."

There is conflict in us all, different animals if you will. Some are positive, some negative, some good some bad, it's a power struggle for control of your mind, soul, which influences actions. The strongest is the one we feed the most. My demons are fed more often than my angels.

In the bible in the book of Genesis, Satan is a snake, in the beginning. In the last book, the book of Revelation, Satan is a mighty serpent. How did he grow? How did he become so powerful?

Since Sweet Pea had spoken to me on speaker with Coffee present I didn't feel it would be a problem if they met. But I was not going to let her meet the others. Coffee was an outsider and I still wasn't too comfortable with this whole project. I had never done anything remotely close to this. I had no prior knowledge of the possible ramifications or repercussions of such an action.

We were traveling in uncharted waters. Coffee began to write in her memo book again. I knew her real name couldn't be Coffee. I didn't care to ask. She felt the need to use an obvious alias.

"Has Cheyanne ever worked for you?" Coffee asked out of the blue.

"No, not in the capacity in which you're asking. I manage her career. She is a member of The Royal Family but not everyone does everything. Each posses their own specific talents and abilities. She's a retired porn-star, singer, actress, writer/relationship sexpert if you will. She's my best friend and someone I Trust."

"Oh, I just wanted to know."

We got to Sweet Pea's apartment.

"Just wait in the car" I mumbled softly to Coffee as I exited the vehicle. As usual the music was blasting so I had to knock hard. She didn't answer so I used my key.

"Oh shit! Mickey, you scared me" said Sweet Pea who was coming out of the shower.

She put on a green terrycloth robe and handed me what looked to be over two grand in mostly small bills.

"I had a regular stop by this morning." She said to explain why there's more than usual. Just at that moment there was a knock at the door.

"Hello is Mickey here?" I looked over my shoulder and it was Coffee.

Sweet Pea didn't recognize Coffee. She didn't know whether to say I was there or not. For the situation and location Coffee was properly dressed. I could have sworn I told Coffee specifically to stay in the car. This is the second time I told her to do something and she altered my instructions. I had to remind myself that Coffee was not one of my wives.

She doesn't work for me. This would be an awkward moment if I weren't Mickey Royal. But Coffee's unexpected arrival came at a most inopportune time. Sweet Pea stepped back as I stepped up.

"Come in, Coffee, Sweet Pea, Sweet Pea this here's Coffee."

"Hey"

"Hello"

I pointed at the couch and Coffee sat down.

"You got the schedule for tonight right?" I asked Sweet Pea.

"Daddy I figured a usual Saturday night. Cleopatra and Glamour mentioned something about a bachelor party.

"I'll get with them later" I replied.

I could see Coffee's wheels turning as she attempted to count my money in her head.

She was literally counting on her fingers and her lips were moving. Sweet Pea kept looking into my eyes as I spoke, periodically glancing over at Coffee. She didn't know who she was. Coffee was dressed like a Royal Family member but was not introduced as such. Coffee was busy looking around Sweet Pea's apartment taking economic inventory.

"I have a date coming in a few daddy" Sweet Pea said.

"We were leaving anyway" I replied.

I pointed at Coffee with my index finger signaled her to stand up. I didn't like how Sweet Pea cut me off about her date coming by as if she was putting us out. So I had to counter as if leaving was still my idea. The power lies behind choice and the balance of power must always be dictated by me.

As Coffee and I walked down the stairs I could see a Caucasian gentleman getting out of what appeared to be an old brown hatchback. He looked down at a slip of paper then looked up again then back down. He was obviously verifying an address on his paper with where he was. It was safe to assume he was her expected date/client. He looked out of place in this neighborhood.

We left and I still needed to collect. Coffee looked as if she's working with us. She looks the part but lacks the charisma to play it. I couldn't risk collecting with Coffee with me. She doesn't know what to and what not to say. I can't charge it to the game and accuse her of being out of pocket because she's a civilian. She's not required to stay in pocket nor does she know how.

"I'm gonna drop you off at your boyfriends house to get some things."

"Ex! Ex-boyfriend! I can't go over there dressed like this."

"Like what?"

"Like a Working girl."

Coffee using her fingers to show sarcastic quotation marks when she said, 'Working girl.'

"So, you have Sweet Pea, Cleopatra, Glamour, and who else is down with Mr. Micky Royal hmmm?" Coffee asked smiling.

Before I could answer her, she pulled out that memo book and began to write again. I don't repeat myself so I said nothing.

"Women have come and gone in my life. Women have come and stayed. I teach my lessons, I never count the students. It's irrelevant to the curriculum."

I didn't fault Sweet Pea for speaking in front of Coffee. She was dressed like a fresh turn out. It was safe to assume Coffee was a potential family member. There was no violation from anyone. Just a collision of worlds with collateral damage.

An accurate assessment of the aftermath of today's events can only be measured in time throughout the day. For every action, there's an equal and opposite reaction so says the laws of physics. The question remains how the Coffee interlude will affect the delicate balance of power with Sweet Pea.

Sweet Pea has been with me for many years. She would never gossip or spread business concerning me or any others. But I knew I'd get a phone call from her with questions attached.

"Where are we going now?" Coffee asked.

"Where I'm taking you sweetheart" I answered.

Sweet Pea called right when I left. I let the phone ring three times before I answered again on speaker.

"Yes?"

" I need to boogie by the beach ok?"

"Ok."

"24 to 36 okay?"

"Yep" I replied.

"Do I dare ask?" asked Coffee.
I turned up the radio and continued driving.

"Sweet Pea asked to use the marina spot for 26 hours max and I agreed. We have a family rule. We don't discuss anything over the phone that we wouldn't want the world to hear. Sweet Pea is a veteran despite what her name implies. She needs no coaching, no prepping, no warnings" I explained to Coffee.

I needed to collect but it could wait. I dedicated this weekend for Coffee's project. I gave Cheyanne my word but it was cramping my style just a little. But I did so enjoy Coffee's company.

"Do I talk too much?"

My fangs drip at the sound of self-evaluating questions. Coffee was unknowingly falling into a pre-spun web that permanently orbits those in the Izm. The size of the web depends on the depth of the Izm that dwells within the individual. As much as I attempted to control it the power seeps through.

"No Coffee you don't talk too much, why do you say that?" I asked to measure the depth of her insecurities only to use them against her for my personal gain at a later date.

"I just don't want to get on your nerves. I really appreciate you doing this for me." Coffee said smiling and leaning into me.

This was the first time there was physical contact between us. I could see peripherally that she was looking at me. Smiling at me, waiting for me to acknowledge her touch. I did not. I kept my head straight driving with tonight's activities on my mind. Coffee had tasted the Izm and liked it. I was trying to protect her from Mickey Royal and the evil that flows through my veins.

"Can you take me to get my things."

"Look, I don't get involved in relationship shit. That's domestic."

"Please, please, Pleeeaaaase!!?" Coffee beggingly cutting me off in mid-sentence.

This time touching me again gripping my arm tight and smiling. I had no choice but to say yes. Coffee was attempting to use her femininity and a hint of sexuality to get a personal favor from a man (Me). Exactly on course. Why disappoint her soul when it can be used in servitude to me. It will teach her she has the power of persuasion through properly placed flirtatious behavior.

"When you ask like that cookie how can I say no" I replied with my usual wry grin.

As we got closer to this ex-boyfriend's house Coffee began to get nervous. She became more talkative. Actually grabbing me around the arm on several occasions. I noticed the closer we got to our destination the tighter her grip. Coffee placed a phone call to let him know that she was coming by. Then her mood went from manic to quiet. I could tell she was pondering the what if factor. Coffee's 22 years old. I've see this movie before. She hasn't. I didn't speak when she stopped speaking. I wanted to see which cards she played.

When we arrived, her clothes were all over the street and sidewalk. She hopped out of the car yelling and screaming at him. Coffee had forgotten how she was dressed. Her ex-boyfriend stopped in his tracks in shock by her attire. I got out of the car slowly taking the long way around. I needed to scope the scene. These are the situations I purposely avoid.

"Coffee bet back in the car," I ordered her.

She hesitated and got in the car. I calmly picked up what I saw and placed two arms full of clothing in my trunk. Her ex-boyfriend was yelling and so was she from the window of my car. I made eye contact with the young man which was enough to make him lower his voice and go back inside their apartment. As we drove off Coffee was crying.

"I hate him, just take me home."

"And where is that?"

She thought about it and her crying intensified. I took her to a spot I had rented in the Hollywood Hills.

It was a four-bedroom mini mansion. I used for swinger parties. No one lived in it consistently. I once operated a bordello out of there with two ladies occupying each room. For VIP swinging couples, I needed a swank location for such activities. I didn't remember what condition I had left the place in so I warned her in advance.

"I'm taking you to a safe place for you to unwind."

"I'm okay"

"No, you're not. Mascara running all down your face."

Coffee burst out in laughter with her tear stained face. By the time we pulled up Coffee was an emotional wreck. She looked bewildered and exhausted.

"Wow is this where you live?"

"I used to but then I found a better use for it other than slumber."

"You speak funny. Not funny but different. Unlike any man I've ever known"

"Is that a compliment or insult?" I asked.

"Definitely a compliment"

"Oh, then I guess that's pretty cool" I replied.

Dummying down my dialect just a tad to make a connection with her of a mutual nature. She has been looking up since we met. It was time to look eye to eye.

When we walked in the place it was clean but virtually empty. There were pictures on the wall all sex related. Condoms and sex toys everywhere. The pool hadn't been skimmed since the last party. The bedrooms were clean. The house contained spotless areas and areas that appeared recently had been lived in.

I escorted her to the civilized portion of the house where she would be staying. I went back outside to retrieve her clothes from the trunk. She had a few pairs of pants, a few shirts and a couple of dresses. I opened a bottle of wine and fired up the jacuzzi.

"I've never met anyone like you before."

"How would you?"

My responses are designed to create more questions than answers at the same time remaining rhetorical. The more answers she thinks she has the more questions she creates for herself, perpetuating her own mystery.

We both got into the hot tub and sipped wine as the sun set. I could feel the conflict raging inside of Coffee's 22-year-old mind. Her body is relaxing as her soul has become entangled in desire. What happens to a spirit who loves what its suppose to hate? What happens when you develop a need to protect that which you're programmed to hate?

"Can I kiss you?" Coffee asked me out of the blue.

She was asking my permission to unlock and act on her own desires. Giving me the keys to her car in a manner of speaking. I didn't answer. I looked into her beautifully innocent eyes with a slight grin.

"I'm sorry, I shouldn't have said that" she stated before I could respond.

Much like in Aikido (a martial arts style) I use the aggressor's momentum against them by simply applying the universal law of transference.

"Sorry to me you said it? Or are you sorry to yourself for feeling it?"

Coffee leaned forward and kissed me on my left cheek, then a peck on the lips.

"Let's fire up the hot tub."

"Hell yeah" Coffee replied.

Coffee disrobed totally and got into the hot tub nude. I got in the tub after her holding a bottle of wine and two glasses. Before Coffee could make a sexual move, I interrupted.

"Tell me about your project?"

"My notes are extensive, the paper is coming along fine."

"Relax, you've had a long day" Since we were in the Hollywood Hills already I had decided to hit Hollywood Blvd with Coffee.

"This is the life, I mean this is living" said Coffee as she tipped her head back and closed her yes.

"Tell me your story Mr. Royal?"

"What's to tell? I'm just a traveling man crossing the burning sands"

"You speak in riddles. I find that so sexy. I find you sexy. Do you think I'm pretty?"

I didn't like where she was going with this conversation. Coffee was getting wetter than the water we were sitting in. My phone which was on top of our pile of clothing began to ring.
I answered on speaker as usual. It was Charlotte Web. I named her that because she catches tricks like a spider catches flies.
She drains them for everything they have then leaves them high and dry.

"Speak"

"Just checking in daddy. Are you coming to see me later?"

"I'm wrapped up for a few days."

"Unwrap and come see me. I'm pregnant."

"How many months?"

"Close to 7 and a half. I need to give birth before I miscarry."

"Copy that" I replied before hanging up.

Coffee's mouth was open. She was trying to digest what she just heard. I'm wrapped up is code for I'm busy, my hands are tied and I can't presently get away. I'm pregnant means I'm holding your money. 7½ months means $7,500. To give birth means for me to come pick it up. Miscarry means to do something foolish with the money. A cellphone on speaker, we must have our own language.

It's common practice for me to keep all of my family calls under a minute. I could see Coffee pondering the meanings in Charlotte's messages. Her demeanor turned cold when she heard the word pregnant. From the position of her eyes and head and the sudden change in her breathing pattern I knew her thoughts. Skills I developed over decades of training from having a shaman for a father. Not to mention a background in hypnosis I long since made the control of the mind my life's work.

Coffee was as easy to read as a See Spot Run book. The goal is to erase her mental chalkboard and begin to write a new lesson without

her being consciously aware of the transformation.
After Charlotte hung up there was an uncomfortable
silence. In these moments I strive. I watched her
mentally search for the words. What to say? What
not to say? Do I wait til he speaks first to reset the
tone?

"Come to me" I ordered.

Coffee obeyed without hesitation. She sat close
enough to me where her legs were draped across
mines. Still, the look on her face was a look of
bewilderedness. I didn't wish to conduct business in
front of Coffee. I had people to see, stops to make
and money to pick up. None of which I wished to
do in front of Coffee.
            I still don't trust her and a week or weekend
wouldn't provide enough time for anything to
develop. Why water a plant that doesn't possess the
ability to grow? That would be a waste of my time.
Time is the only none redeemable universal
element. Every moment I spend with Coffee I'm not
spending with the Royal Family. I allowed Coffee
to rest her head upon my shoulder. She had a need
to feel protected apparently at that particular
moment. Women don't love men who love them.
Women love men who love themselves. I am the
living manifestation of this truth.
            Coffee began to nibble on my ear with soft
dry multiple kisses. It was now officially time to go.

"Are you ready"

Pimping Ain't Easy

"Ready for what?" Coffee replied with a smile.

"I don't know sweetheart. I don't work from a script. I make this shit up as I go."

"What shit is that Mr. Royal?"

"Life Coffee, life. We're all here for the first time and only here once. Tragic is the life predestined. Expect the unexpected."

We got out of the hot tub just as the sun went down. The view of the sunset's cascading silhouette behind the Hollywood sign caught Coffee's eye momentarily stopping her in her tracks. We went back in the house and Coffee began looking through her pile of clothes for suitable attire.
I went to the kitchen to retrieve a trash bag for her to put her clothes in.

"Here we won't be coming back here."

The family had a swinger's weekend pool splash bash scheduled in ten days.
It was important that I left the house in the same condition it was in when we entered. Coffee had on a dress and seemed to be relaxed. We drove down the hill and around the curvy road til we hit Western Ave. We made a right on Sunset Blvd.

"This was once the most famous and productive track in the country."

67

Mickey Royal

"It's not anymore?"

"No" I answered as Coffee began once again writing in her memo book.

Different tracks produce different results. No two tracks are the same. I knew what she wanted to see but my game is on another level altogether. I am to teach my wives everything they know, not everything I know. As we drove down Sunset I pointed out 'hot spots' where hookers once stood now occupied by meth heads. I made a left on La Cienega and hit the downhill slope.

"You see that club billboard live?"

"Yes"

"Before it was billboard live it was called Gizzaries. This was in 1990. That was one of my spots back then. Also, the Roxy next door."

"That where you hung out?"

"That's where my brother and I used to sell powder cocaine. We were kids then."

"You are too much Mickey."

I didn't respond because no response was needed. Coffee started to rub my leg but not in a sexual way. She rested her hand on my thigh. She began to pick lint from my pants. She leaned over to kiss my cheek yet again. We made a left on Santa Monica Blvd. As we drove up Santa Monica, I started again to feel more of a tour guide again.

"When we cross La Brea ave you'll notice that the hookers are a lot taller than most women."

"Why is that?"

"Because they're men. This is the only transsexual track in the world."

"Do the customers know they're men?"

"Yes, the tricks know. This track stops at Van Ness avenue."

Just when Coffee began to become comfortably familiar with me a new element was introduced. Unexpected information or turn of events returned the awkward silence. Her uncomfortableness is my comfort zone. Great power dwells in anonymity.

"How come we haven't met your ladies? This Royal Family of yours? Now there's Sweet Pea, Charlotte something, Glamour, Cleopatra, and who else? I mean how many others?"

"What are you doing Barbara Walters, taking roll?" I replied jokingly but her questioning created unnoticeable distance between us.

I didn't trust cookie or her memo book. But I gave my word and the loyal Mickey Royal always keeps his word. My phone rang interrupting our banter. It was an old friend, Freeway Rick Ross.

He had gotten out of prison after almost 20 years. He was set up and wrongfully accused by the CIA. He's known for being one of the biggest drug dealer in America. He was having a coming home party in Long Beach.

"Mick"

"What's up?"

"This Rick. Hey you coming?"

I didn't plan on attending because Cookie was with me but I wasn't going to tell him no.

"Yeah, text me the address."

"Alright."

"Coffee slight change in plan. We're going to a family get together. Make sure you leave that memo book of yours in the car."

"Why?"

Just as we stopped at a red light before hitting the freeway I looked at her. Before I could respond she retracted.

"Alright Mickey, my bad I'm sorry."

I wrote her insubordination as being 22. As we drove to the hotel ballroom I explained to her who exactly Freeway Rick is and was. Coffee's speech patterns had changed after I briefed her on how to carry herself with me. Normally an event such as this I'd be with Cheyanne Foxx aka my life partner. But I figured as long as Mickey Royal author of The Pimp Game series didn't show up stag it wouldn't be too detrimental to my reputation. Coffee was desperately trying not to show how nervous she was but she was nervous. I could hear a slight tremble in her voice.

"Shhh Coffee, we're here."

"What do I say?"

"Nothing"

I told Coffee as we exited the car. I could tell she was thrilled to be included.
She humbly walked close to me. We were first greeted by Rick's wife.

"Hey Mickey, you made it."

"I wouldn't have missed this for the world."

She escorted us to our seats. I didn't know or recognize anyone. I was sitting with. A few minutes later Rick walks in with a few gentlemen I didn't recognize. I didn't say a word. I make a point not to speak in front of strangers. As soon as Rick walked in he began shaking hands and answering questions. From the conversation at the table that I was listening to, but not participating in, it was safe to assume they were in the media business in some way. They were speaking to each other and periodically looking at me, the silent one. As soon as Rick noticed me he came right over.

"What's happening?" I said as I stood up from my seat and hugged him.

"Just blessed brother" he responded with a smile on his face.

As we began to speak Coffee reaches into her purse and retrieved a camera. Without permission, she snapped our picture together. We spoke a while longer then he kept it moving. He made his way to the podium and gave a speech as the guest of honor. When he finished the music came on. People began to dance.
"Dance with me" Coffee said while pulling me onto the dancefloor.

I didn't know how Rick would react to the unexpected snapshot. When I looked over Coffee's shoulder I saw him smiling and dancing with his wife so it was all good. Coffee was quite the dancer. I enjoyed watching her move. We danced to one song and I made my way over to Rick, thanked him for the invite and we left. I come late and leave early. That's always been my style.

"Why didn't you want to stay and socialize?"

"Because I'm anti-social."

"You are a real-life vampire."

"Vampires are technically dead so that's an oxymoron."

I opened the door gentlemanly for Coffee, looked around before getting in, then left. I am here to support a friend. Events such as these are not my M.O. But neither is being a tour guide. I needed to place Coffee somewhere and check a few traps. I needed to make calls I didn't want her to hear.
I needed to meet with people that I didn't want her meeting. Coffee doesn't understand whenever you meet someone that you've interrupted a life in progress. My entire routine has been thrown off by her.

"You live an exciting life Mr. Royal."

"Really, funny you should say that because I find it quite boring. I've always been me so I have nothing to compare it to."

Tonight was business as usual. I had much activity in the machine loaded. I had a swing party in the hills, a bachelor party at the penthouse suite of the Radisson and in-calls at the marina spot. Money was being generated as fast as my wheels were turning.

"That was fun Mickey. What did you and Rick discuss?"

"Can you keep a secret?"

"Yes"

"So can I."

Coffee leaned over and kissed me on the right side of my cheek. Realizing that her questioning has become a bit nerve-wracking. As expected, out comes the memo pad. I can only imagine the notes she was taking. If I didn't give her the answers she wanted was she making things up? Incriminating things. I had pictures of her back at the marina spot but I needed more. I still didn't trust her.

"What was Cheyanne Foxx doing when I pulled up?"

"Writing, working on an erotic novel or some kind of book on her computer. I tried to read over her shoulder but couldn't see anything. Why do you ask?"

"Because I wanted to know the answer."

"Your answers leave me more puzzled than questions" Coffee said as she laughed.

Coffee seemed to be having the time of her life with me. I on the other hand had enough of Ms. Coffee and her memo book. We had no particular place to go. I had a tank full of gas and a pocket full of money. My wives know how to hold it down when a player's not around.

"Let's go to dinner, in Tijuana."

"What you mean, Mexico?"

"No, Tijuana Arizona... Of course, Mexico Coffee."

I reached into the center console to retrieve my cigarette holder. Inside I kept five pre-rolled marijuana blunts. I didn't know nor care how Coffee felt about the smoke. I put in a CD and began playing the song Let the Music Play by Shannon.
"Hey, now where' talking!" shouted Coffee.

I didn't know if her excitement was for the music or the weed. Coffee just looked at me in awe as I drove down the 405 Freeway. I could see her out of the corner of my eye.

"I have nothing to wear"

"Yes you do Coffee. Remember you have a bag full of clothes in the trunk."

"Oh yea, that's right but what about you?"

Coffee was unfamiliar with the game, the life in general. In the trunk of my cars at all times I kept an escape bag. That bag stays packed with three outfits, 3,500 dollars or so, and a passport. In my line of work or life or lifestyle everyone must be prepared to disappear or lay low at any given time. I had a little over 1,100 dollars in my pocket.

"I'll be ok Coffee. I have clothes in the trunk, too" I replied. After hitting the blunt 4 times Coffee spoke up.

"Hey brotha, puff puff pass. You know what's up."

I was pleased to find out Coffee wasn't a total square. I still didn't trust her. I noticed that as we smoked the more talkative cookie was. We were smoking some top shelf sativa. We were flying down the freeway doing 75 MPH with no one in front of us or behind us. Both windows, driver and passenger were slightly cracked so the car wouldn't reek of marijuana. I appreciated Coffee's spontaneous free-spirited nature.
She reminded me a lot of Cheyanne in a way. I enjoyed showing Coffee things she's never seen. Taking her to places she's never been. I hadn't decided yet if we would stop in San Diego and get a room then go into Tijuana in the morning. Or if I

would just push it straight through. It depended how sleepy I was when we hit Oceanside which I would consider the halfway point.

"Your life is like a non-stop episode of Pulp Fiction. I mean your everyday life makes mines look like I don't live at all."

"Life is a blank page, Coffee. If you don't like the story, complain to the author."

"Oh, it's my fault I'm boring?"

"Coffee you're far from boring"

"When do I get to see some pimping?!"

"Hopefully never. I'm here to translate and explain what you see and hear. I've been purposely keeping you out of harms way."

"Really, by introducing me to Freeway Ricky Ross. I mean The Real One."

"I didn't introduce you to anyone. You interrupted our conversation by snapping a picture. But it's all good though."

"Oh, was I out of pocket?" asked Coffee sardonically in an attempt to show me she's not as green as she thinks I think she is. Not fully understanding the Izm she has no chance to get inside my head when I'm currently in hers. My

weapon of choice is between my ears, not my legs
nor between my mattress (referring to my gun).
We were both wide awake smoking blunt
after blunt. Coffee was high as a kite and I was
feeling nice. By the way she smoked, I knew it
wasn't her first time. From her periodic coughing
and rapid speech I knew she wasn't used to the
quality of weed I smoked.

"I can see why women love you."

"Women or you?" Coffee paused just long enough
to deflect.

"Thank you for today, with my ex."

"Don't mention it. It's what I do."

"What, rescue women?"

"Yes, from themselves."

"I hate when you do that."

"Do what Coffee?"

"Answer my questions and make me think. Stop
that" said Coffee jokingly as she slapped my thigh.

Then she slowly rubbed my leg and said,

"Your music taste is weird."

"Then its befitting cause I'm weird." I noticed Coffee didn't write in that book when she was getting high. I like a more relaxed Coffee.

"Now were in Oceanside."

I gave Coffee a brief history lesson about the city of Oceanside and its significance in the history of the Pimp Game. Every pimp getting his feet wet has to hit Oceanside twice a month. Its where Camp Pendleton Marine base is. It wasn't just a training camp for marines. It was a training ground for pimps with up and coming stables.

Every payday we'd come down in two car loads and work. My weapons in those days were anonymity and discretion. In situations with celebrities, military, conventions or any high profiled arena it's how you do something as opposed to what you do. My ladies would be dressed conservatively, hitting the clubs, adult book stores, and service bars etc.

The track here was indoor and everyone knew who we were and why we were there. Our presence was felt but not seen. Operating below the radar outside the danger zone. I even had an LLC which took 3rd party checks. Some of them would actually sign over complete checks to the company. It's always safer when the trick has more to lose than the ho.

Because of the program my organization ran we never had a glitch. Also, it is expected as an unwritten rule in the game that you protect the client's identity at all cost. A reputation takes a lifetime of consistently to build and one mistake to ruin. Our reputations remain intact until this very day.

Impressing and mesmerizing Coffee offered no challenge to me at all. It was nothing in it for me other than gaining yet another cheerleader. Having my ego stroked does nothing for me.

It was cute to watch her ponder on what makes Mickey tick. Her shovel was too dull to dig into my brain. She was smart for 22 but not wise. Wisdom comes with time and experience. Knowledge, wisdom, and understanding of the Shadow World Coffee couldn't possibly grasp in a week or weekend.

I recklessly enjoyed toying with her.

"Didn't your parents ever tell you not to ride with strangers?"

"You're not a stranger Mickey."

"Coffee my dear, they don't come any stranger."

I decided to drive straight into Tijuana, Mexico.

"We were actually in Mexico. I've never been to another country."

Coffee began snapping pictures like a typical tourist. I enjoyed watching her enjoy herself. Her mouth was gaped open so wide I was worried a fly might fly in it. We drove up a hill and parked.

There was hip-hop music being played so we went to a club on Revolucion' Ave.

"Do you speak Spanish?" asked Coffee.

"Not at the moment."

We went inside the club only to discover that it was too crowded. The wait was five to ten minutes for a table. The maître 'd came over to us.

"Right this way. We have a table on the balcony for the happy couple."

Coffee didn't bother to correct the gentleman. But I noticed her looking and smiling as we made our way to the balcony.

"What a lovely view" said Coffee.

"Yes, it is, I love this town."

We were under a heat lamp so we both were warm. Besides we both were wearing jackets. I politely ordered margaritas for the both of us. One of the men, a bartender I presume, came over with a funnel and whispered in Coffee's ear. Coffee said;

"Hell yeah!"

And the next thing I knew he had tipped her head back, stuck a funnel in her mouth and began to pour beer and tequila down her throat. Everyone started screaming;

"Go! Go! Go!"

Then he grabbed her by the head and shook it while blowing a loud whistle in her ear. When he finished he placed what appeared to resemble Mardi Gras beads. Coffee was beyond tipsy at this point. Actually borderline drunk, slightly incoherent and high off strong marijuana in a foreign country with a pimp. This is the part when she should subconsciously thank God she knows Cheyanne Foxx. Coffee has turned 180 degrees in front of her own eyes without seeing a thing.

"Woah, that shit was intense, oh, oh my"

"Coffee are you okay sweetheart? You're not about to toss your cookies are you?"

Coffee didn't answer. She was still visibly dizzy. I dined sufficiently on two fish tacos. We sat there and conversated a bit. She grew more talkative as her inebriation levels increased. Between the five blunts we smoked on the way down here combined with her recent alcohol explosion Coffee was traveling in the stratosphere.

The lakes and rivers of manipulation and deceit are not unfamiliar nor uncharted waters for me. I have sailed and navigated well threw them over my lifespan. I mercifully ordered Coffee a large coffee. I didn't want her staggering down the street, slurring her words while leaning on my shoulder. I was prepared to sit as long as it took til Coffee sobered up enough to be good company again.

I was enjoying the view over her shoulder. Coffee was slowly drinking, sobering up from the coffee.

"Dance with me Coffee."

We stood up and I wrapped my arms around her from behind. She firmly placed her hands on my hands which were around her waist. This was the first time I had initiated touch between us. It was well received. As we looked out upon the well-lit city;

"Isn't the view beautiful?" Coffee softly spoke.

I slowly spun her around so our eyes met.

"It certainly is" I firmly responded.

Then I slowly turning her back to her original position. My pelvis pressed firmly against her butt. Her hair smelled of cherry bark and almonds. I kissed her gently behind the ear as we swayed back and forth to the music. Coffee tilted her head exposing more of her neck. Inviting this vampire took take yet a deeper bit. Instead I whispered in her ear,

"Let's go."

I took her firmly by the wrist and we made our way out of the club in to the street.

We walked along Revolucion' Ave dodging beggars and overzealous salesmen trying to lure us into their establishment.

"How long have you and Cheyanne been friends?" I curiously asked.

"I'm really a friend of her sister's. We grew up together on the same street. Cheyanne always called me her little sister too."

My phone wouldn't ring in Mexico for some strange reason. I couldn't tell if people were calling me or not. I had several things going on in LA, Hollywood Hills, and the Marina. I needed to check on these things but couldn't get to them from where I was. Even so, my wives are well trained and more than capable of holding it down my absence. We've been forced to be separated on numerous occasions for longer periods of time due to my unfortunate incarcerations. But still I felt I was needed on the turf. I hailed a cab for us.

"Where to?" the cabdriver asked.

"Mickey, something tells me this isn't your first time."
"Sweetheart, I've never had a first time."

"Excuse me Mr. Professional" Coffee said as she gave me an innocent re-assuring kiss on the cheek.

The human mind has been my canvas in which I've
painted for years. Behavioral science, why people
do what they do. When you understand the why's,
you analyze the how's, to manipulate the who's and
when's, only to determine the what's.
        We arrived at club New York. It's ironic to
catch a cab to club New York in Tijuana Mexico
and I can't hail a cab in New York city.

"You really know your way around."

I grabbed her around the wrist and we went inside.
Club New York is a bar/strip club. We sat in a
quaint little dark corner, just the two of us. A
waitress immediately came over to take our order.

"I'll have a shot of bourbon straight. "And for the
lady?"

"Sex on the beach." Coffee answered while staring
into my eyes.

        I wanted to tell her so bad, I get it! You
wish to ride space mountain so to speak. I found
her juvenile flirtatious advances flattering. I didn't
want Coffee to get drunk, again. It's not my style to
liquor up a woman then take advantage of her.
I turn them on, turn them up, then turn them out
with their permission. Coffee danced over to the
stage with drink in hand and tipped the dancer 5
dollars.

"Coffee, follow me."

We went upstairs in the VIP lounge.

"Why don't you get a lap dance, my treat."

"Okay I'm game" she said.

At first Coffee was nervous but quickly loosened
up. She was very comfortable with half naked
women touching her all over. Typical college girl in
the prime of her sexual explorative stage. I could
tell she had been with women before.
        As the stripper was finishing up her dance,
Coffee attempted to suck the strippers left breast.

"No no oh no" the stripper softly said while pushing
back as the song ended.

While Coffee was her lap dance I finished her drink.

"Let's go." I could tell Coffee wanted to stay but
she slowly got up, tipped the lady and we left.

"Where are we?"

"Do you know where we are?"

"I'm never lost Coffee."

We walked down the hill to the end of the block.
We were met by a street vendor selling tacos from a
cart. Being from LA, I'm used to eating lunch even
dinner from catering trucks or push cart street
vendors.

86

"Coffee are you hungry?"

"Starving"

"Let us have four lengua tacos with everything."

"I enjoyed the club," said Coffee.

"I noticed"

"Yeah I saw you looking."

"Looking, it was more like staring" I replied.

Coffee was holding on to my arm. She smiled, chuckled a little, slapped my chest and rubbed it.

"Um this is the best taco I've ever had."

"Well, we ordered Mexican food in Mexico. I mean what do you expect?"

"I know huh" said Coffee.

As we ate and walked to the end of the block we made a left.

"Coffee this is the track. All of the ladies on both sides of the street are working girls, Prostitutes. All of them charge the same price no negotiation, no haggling. 35 dollars American. How it works is like this: You pick a lady and go to the hotel she's standing in front of. The two of you walk up to the window. You hand 35 dollars to your selected lady. She slips 5 dollars under the glass. The lady behind the glass gives her back a key and a condom. You and your selected lady of leisure go to the room numbered on the key."

"Look at all of these policemen. Aren't the girls afraid of getting busted?"

"Remember you're in a socialist country, not a nanny state. The police are patrolling on foot to serve as protection for the ladies, not to arrest them. The cab drivers stay posted. Parked outside the hotels ready to take the American tricks back to their original location. This system operates around the clock like a well-oiled machine."

Coffee stood there, momentarily mesmerized while she paid close attention to the details per mechanism. She watched the rotation pointing out exactly step by step as I just described.

"Oh my God you're right."

"Oh my God, you sound surprised" I mockingly repeated.

We slowly walked down the street arm in arm. Slowly because that was Coffee's chosen pace.
I guess she wanted a closer look. The ladies all looked beautiful. Their ages ranging from 18 to 25 or so it appeared.

"Taxi! Let's bounce sweetheart."

We headed back to Revolucion' Ave.

"That was fun" said Coffee.

Before we left we went into a smoke shop to purchase some Cuban cigars. We walked a little further to a pharmacia. Coffee was hanging on my every move. We purchased 1,000 valium at $0.50 a pill.

"Now it's time to go."

We made our way back to the parking lot and left. Usually when I make these runs there's a line to get back into the US. The line can take from 30 minutes to 3 hours depending on the time of day. Since we were a few hours from daybreak there was no line. We just drove straight threw without stopping. They have a checkpoint to go through but when you drive back they just ask one or two questions then pass you through.

We were now headed back to the marina. I figured it was vacant now. Coffee fell asleep on the way. I was also sleepy but decided to keep pushing it. I had two hours in front of me and my passenger was knocked out. I rolled down the window so the cold air could assist with keeping me up.

It only worked temporarily. As my eyes got heavier I decided to pull off the Highway in Dana Point.

Dana Point is an expensive beach front community. As soon as you exit the highway, you're bombarded with surf board shops. I drove and stopped at the first motel I saw. Coffee was literally snoring. I felt guilty for having to wake her up just to go back to sleep. Didn't seem to make sense to me. So I left her in the car with her window cracked and a note on the steering wheel which read 'I'm in room 109.' I went inside and just passed out.

Maybe I could have made it back to LA but I didn't want to chance it. Besides this gave me a chance to catch up on some phone calls. I called around to touch base with the Royal Family first. Everyone was on point and where they needed to be except Sweet Pea. She and I knew better than to text one another so I just left a coded message.

"Hello girl just left the park, had to walk my dog, call me."

We never use names. The use of the word 'girl' lets her know I'm talking specifically to her. If I said, 'walk the dog' that would mean our business. 'My dog' implies this personal business of mines. The dog references how important this business was. The usage of the word "had" is to imply an unavoidable obligation.

As the sun began to rise, like any vampire it was time for me to sleep. I took the top cover off the bed and hung it over the curtain to totally block out the sun. I took a nice hot bath and shower and called it a night, or should I say day.

Charlotte Web

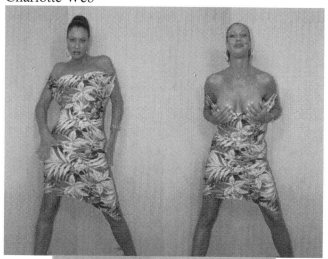

Freeway Ricky Ross(The real one, not the rapper on
the left), Mickey Royal(right)

Mickey Royal

Chapter 3
Monday, March 17th

I must have been more exhausted than I expected because I was awakened by Coffee giving me a blow job. I watched her for close to a minute. I was so tired I guess the message took its own time reaching the brain.

"Stop" I gently said as I rubbed my fingers through her hair.

"What's wrong, you don't like it?"

"How would I know? I was asleep."

"I can finish" Coffee said as she laid there next to me.

"You are finished. We need to be heading back."

Usually nothing takes me by surprise, but I must say she did. I knew she was trapped in the Izm. I actually expected her to make her move tonight. The ambiance of the Izm had her acting on her attraction ahead of schedule. My slight rejection of Coffee placed an uncomfortable silence between us. I enjoyed watching Coffee's attempt at back pedaling after such an aggressive move. Normally I'm used to dealing with women from the life. Women from the life possess more inner confidence. I enjoyed watching her search for a sign of affirmation in me.

I remember as a child we had a mouse loose in the house. My parents set traps with no success. We had a cat named Sassy. One day when I came home from school I saw Sassy hiding in the corner. She seemed to be busy so I investigated. I saw her with the mouse. She had bitten off one of the mouse legs and taken a small chunk out of it. Sassy wasn't trying to eat the mouse. At least not yet. Sassy seemed to be amusing herself by slapping the mouse with her paws, letting it crawl away then pulling it back. Sassy had developed a game at the mouse's expense.

As we got into the car I couldn't help but notice that Coffee was less talkative. She struggled within herself and it was visibly obvious. Her conscience mind wanting to make eye contact with me but when she did her subconscious mind, still processing the rejection, lowered her head and eyes. There was silence for miles. I sensed she was waiting on me to address it, wondering did she screw up? What must he think of me? Questioning herself, her intentions. She began to open up as we entered the outskirts of LA County.

"Look Mickey, I'm sorry about that whole misunderstanding back at the room. I mean, I just thought we had made some sort of connection."

"I enjoy your company a great deal Coffee."

I decided to give her an out and slightly redirect her apology into an offbeat compliment, thus breaking the tension. Coffee, previously in a slouching position had now sat up and began once again writing in her memo book. Then she slowly started returning to her talkative self.

"Were you at least enjoying though? I mean, do I measure up to your wives?"

"I never compare my wives or women in general at all. I find it tackie and debasing. Every woman I've ever come in contact with was as unique as a fingerprint. The very thought in and of itself is beneath me."

"Would I make a good prostitute?" Coffee asked.

Evidently she had reached the body of her report because her questions now required answers with a little more meat. I asked myself, 'Should I play this game with her?' How far should I go with this? How much fun should I have?' The more 'cat and injured mouse' fun I have with her the more out of character I must become, thus lowering my defenses. Coffee had crossed the familiarity line. But in all fairness, I pulled her close to that line like a sick game of tug of war. Since Coffee took liberties upon me without permission I decided to let her in my world a tad bit deeper. Putting the Ball of power once again in my court. It was my serve. But it always is.

I don't have uncomfortable moments, I create them. Unknowing to Coffee we were headed straight to Charlotte's house. Charlotte Web was one of the smartest women and most skilled hustlers I had ever seen. Charlotte lived in a four-bedroom, three bath, seven hundred thousand dollar home in Sherman Oaks. We pulled up and parked in the driveway.

"Who's house is this? Is it yours?"

"Well, in a manner of speaking, I bought it. I have clothes here."

Not only did I have money to pick up, I wanted Coffee to put faces and lifestyles with the names she had written down. As we approached the door, Coffee noticed that I had my own key. I made her to pay special note of it by shaking and rattling my keys before we entered.

There are no coincidences in this life and fate is unpredictable, uncontrollable. Everything I do is done by design. I always pay close attention to the fact that I'm being paid close attention to at all times.

The journey can't be separate from the destination.
They're both symbiotically connected. We walked
in and I announced myself as always. Charlotte
Web could be working.

"Honey, I'm home"

     Charlotte came from out of the shower with
nothing but a towel wrapped around her. Coffee's
eyes were as wide as her nose. She was looking all
around Charlottes living room taking obvious
detailed notes. Literally itemizing the inventory, just
as I expected. As Charlotte leaped into my arms
hugging me I spun her around so Coffee would
notice her towel was also Egyptian cotton just like
the ones in the marina spot. That way she could feel
my presence and see my flag. I'm everywhere and
nowhere at the same time.

"I got a brick for you"

"Then hit me in the head with it so I can add it to
the wall" I answered.

     A brick means 10,000 dollars in our coded
language. Hit me in the head with it just means give
it to me now. Add it to the wall means it's being
legally invested. The wall is our family's ongoing
project. An LLC that the lifetime family members
all have an equal share on the board of trustees. We
as a conglomerate unify our purchasing power to
open and establish businesses of a wide variety.
From real-estate, to restaurants, and anything in

between. Specializing primarily in low risk, high return ventures.

"Charlotte this is Coffee, Coffee this is Charlotte Web, my wife."

"Your wife?!" Coffee's jealously responded.

Charlotte licked my cheek and said

"One of them honey" to Coffee.

Coffee was shocked at Charlotte's beauty, success and cheerful attitude. I knew if she needed a visible representation of life in the Pimp Game then Ms. Web was perfect. Charlotte's home was covered in self-portraits. She was a teenage model who became an Oakland Raiders cheerleader. She was no stranger to around the world cruises, exotic sports cars, and high-profile clients.

Charlotte wasn't for rent, she was for lease with implied option to buy. She possessed the skills, background and finesse for the long slow con. She didn't work hard she worked smart. Charlotte excused herself to put on a kimono and came back out. She's as sexy as Marilyn Monroe. Tough as Virginia Hill, elegant as Lena Horne, and as quick witted as Mae West. Her home was immaculately decorated which certainly appealed to her upscale clientele whom appreciated her discretion and grace.

100

"What brings you to this neck of the woods besides me?"

"Just you Ms Web" I replied.

"Little ole me? Well I do declare" answered Charlotte in an exaggerated southern drawl.

Charlotte, Coffee, and myself were in her living room. Everything was white with gold trim matching her kimono and fingernails.

"Honey would you like something to drink?" Charlotte asked.

"What do you have?" Coffee answered.

"Whatever those pretty little lips of yours desire. I recommend anything wet."

"I'll have a soda"

"and?"

"That's all" Coffee replied.

"Oh isn't she precious?" Charlotte said as she excused herself yet again.

She went into the kitchen and came back with a diet 7-Up and a backpack.

"For you honey" said Charlotte. As she handed Coffee the glass.

"Thank you"

"For you baby" said Charlotte as she handed me the backpack.

I wouldn't dare insult Ms Web by looking in the backpack or counting money in front of her. It would also be rude to get up and leave after collecting. I would always sit with Charlotte for a while afterwards. She enjoyed the company. She lived alone in a huge home. Not totally, she had a white cat named Ciao. Ciao wore a 14k gold collar.

"Honey would you like anything else?" Charlotte asked Coffee.

"No thank you, I'm fine" Charlotte walked over to Coffee, rubbed her fingers through her hair and said;

"You sure are." She then looked at me and asked;

"Baby are you going to Cheyanne's pool party?"

"More than likely. I love Cheyanne and I love to swim."

"What about you honey?" Charlotte asked Coffee.

"What? Me? If she invites… Sure… maybe I'll come."

"You'll cum for sure if I'm there, I guarantee" said Charlotte, obviously flirting with Coffee.

Charlotte was great at what she did. Sexuality oozed from her pores. I got up to say goodbye on that note and Coffee followed my lead.

"Well, it was a pleasure meeting you Ms Web."

"Likewise honey, and call me Charlotte or tonight."

I kissed Charlotte passionately on the lips, rubbed her up and down from her back to the butt, then back again, then we left. Charlotte had hit the garage opener for Coffee could see her white Jaguar convertible parked next to her white BMW. Charlotte walked us outside and pretended to be looking for something in the garage. But I knew better. One thing Charlotte loved doing was showing off. Coffee was speechless.

Now Coffee had met Sweet Pea and Charlotte Web. Two totally different females in the same game on the same team but different positions. As soon as we hit the highway Coffee broke out the memo book and began writing. Still, yet not uttering a spoken word.

I felt I needed to regroup so we headed back to the marina. Coffee was silent for most of the way home. Undoubtedly shuffling and arranging the cards she was just dealt. Charlotte is a professional and a lot to take in. She can be a bit intimidating at times. I took advantage of the unexpected silence to make a few phone calls. I had been away a few days so it was high time I reconnected. The first thing I did was listen to my voicemail. Just to make sure if there were any problems or surprises I could catch them early and nip them in the bud.

As a habit I listen to my voicemail on speaker when I'm driving. I'm so use to being in the car alone or just with the Royal Family. I really don't associate with strangers and I'm too old to make new friends. The phrase 'new friends' is an oxymoron. A true friendship needs time to develop. It has a unified heartbeat of its own.

Like a combined separate entity that both parties contribute to similar to a child or business. It goes through trials and tribulations during different stages of development. It has an introduction (birth), honeymoon stage (all is well) etc. It takes time to develop enough trust to where it blossoms into a full-blown friendship. When I checked my messages, I had an assortment of calls. Messages;

"Hello Mister Man. I need to schedule an appointment with Dr. Feel Good. Call me lover!"

"Wow, which wife was that? Coffee asked with a hint of jealousy in her voice.

"That was my lawyer Mrs. Jones" I replied.

"Are you serious?"

Pimping Ain't Easy

"Always."

"Is she a wife too?"

"She's an asset to the family and someone I have business arrangements with. I also enjoy having sex with her when I have time. Why do you ask?"

"Wow...oh...I was just asking...I...I mean she sounded all sexy."

"She is."

Coffee began again writing in her memo book. As we approached the marina spot I noticed that Sweet Pea's car was parked down the street. I didn't know if she was with a client or just cooling out. I text her a message:

"I'm on the beach are you swimming?" The beach was code for the marina. Swimming means are you working with a client currently?

"Just lying on the sand means I'm alone, off duty doing nothing."

"Now we can go upstairs. Don't forget to get your clothes out the trunk" I said to Coffee.

When we walked in I could tell Sweet Pea was surprised to still see me with Coffee. I could sense the tension in the air. Two lionesses circling, sizing

each other up. One feels she must defend what hers.
The other willing to take what she feels is hers.
Both ladies equally beautiful to me in their own
unique way. But Sweet Pea knows she's far more
valuable.

"Hey, Cough Drop was it?" Sweet Pea asked.

"It's Coffee…Coffee."

"Oh…whatever"

I knew Sweet Pea well. She knew her name.
She hadn't forgotten it that quickly. She was being
messy. Throwing shit in the game so to speak. That
was Sweet Pea's way of telling Coffee she wasn't
that important. I made no comment. I went to my
closet and placed the backpack in my safe. That was
my way of saying that I'm far above anything petty
or common.

When I walked in Sweet Pea handed me
1,250 dollars. She knows we pass envelopes. She
wanted cookie to see her value. Sweet Pea
apparently felt threatened by Coffee in some way.
Coffee took her own liberties with the marina spot
and took her clothes to my bedroom. I know that
was for Sweet Pea. They were both behaving quite
territorial.

I went to go take a shower. Also, to listen to
the rest of my messages in private. Besides, I was
curious to see what would happen between the two
with my visible absence.

There's nothing like being at home. Even though technically I don't have a home. I just have several 'spots.' If I had to call one of them home it would be the marina. They say home is where the heart is. I love the water and the view. The environment of the marina is a million miles away from the atmosphere in which we dwell. 'Message 2 beep!;

"Hey Mickey, it's your wife Cheyanne Foxx. I'm headed to Las Vegas for a video shoot. I'll be starring and directing. I know I had retired but they made me an offer I couldn't refuse. Call you when I get there. Also, I'm a few pages from finishing my book. You'll love it. I love you daddy muah,"

'Message 3 beep!;
"Yo Mick, this is Lonzo (Grandmaster Lonzo of the World Class Wreckin Crew). I'm having a soiree tonight. Why don't you fall through. I got you covered VIP all the way doc."

Lonzo calls everyone doc.

'Message 4 beep!;

"Mickey Royal This is Lee Mack (famous player and well known LA pimp). Just inviting you to the Boom Boom Room tonight holla."

The Boom Boom room is Lonzo's club so I just received two invites to the same event.
'Message 5;

"Make up everywhere. Lights, camera, action. I'm ready for my close-up Mr. DeMille."

That was coded message from Glamour. Make up or lipstick means its Glamour. Lights camera action means I'm working hard. Ready for my close up means come pick soon, package ready.

'Beep! you have no more messages;'

I had other plans for tonight. It looks like I'm going to the Boom Boom Room. I would never refuse a personal invite from Lonzo and Lee Mack, two such famous players. A no show would be an insult. I must attend. At least stick my head in, out of respect. I love to travel but I also love checking in with the home front. Just like that my plans for tonight have changed.

The last time I saw Lee Mack he was at Bishop Magic Juan's birthday party a few years back. The World-Famous Players Ball it was. Yea it will be cool to see some of the old gang. Fraternity so to speak, graduates, alumni from sidewalk university. Hell, it may be fun. I haven't had fun in quite some time. Fun doesn't usually fit into my schedule.

When I got out of the shower I put on my monogrammed satin royal blue robe with satin pajamas. I keep it casual in the marina. My neighbors think I'm just a writer who occasionally has beautiful women stay over for short and long periods of time. Discretion has its value.

I walked back into the front room where the
ladies were. Sweet Pea knows how I feel about
street clothes in my house. All of my wives do. In
the home the Royal Family, myself included are to
be leisurely dressed in bedroom attire at all times.

My mood is stress-free and I project that
mood wherever I go. Wherever I am. I decided to
up to ante so to speak. Coffee had knocked down
the first domino by attempting to give me a
blowjob. That gave me the green light to continue to
toy with her yet a little more.

"Coffee why aren't you properly dressed?"

Coffee looked at me in pajamas and Sweet
Pea in black lace lingerie and excused herself to my
bedroom. Coffee came back out with one of my
shirts, no bra, and no panties. Ironically, she was
wearing footsie socks. Sweet Pea then got up and
went to my hallway armoire. That's where I keep
the party favors.

Sweet Pea knows we don't reveal anything
in mixed company. But Sweet Pea was in rare form.
She has seen me with Coffee twice now and still
can't figure out where she fits in our equation.
Sweet Pea came back with the silver platter. She
had 3 shots of tequila, 5 lines of cocaine and 2
marijuana blunts rolled fat and tight. She placed the
platter in front of Coffee.

"Help yourself" Sweet Pea softly said to Coffee.

"After you" Coffee quickly responded as she slowly slid the tray back in front of Sweet Pea.

This was interesting. As I sat there between these ladies I knew what was in Sweet Pea's mind. Either you're about this life or you're not. No spectators, cheerleaders, groupies or fans allowed in the owner's box. Players, coaches and owners only. That's the game, that's the life, our life.

Sweet Pea grabbed a straw and tooted two lines of Peruvian cocaine like a vacuum cleaner. She then took a shot of tequila straight. Sweet Pea then stuck her fingers in the glass and tiled her head back then stuck those fingers in her nostrils. Inhaling the wet tequila drops so that any residue of cocaine left behind would go down her throat. Sweet Pea then pushed the tray in front of Coffee and said,

"Bon appetite."

Coffee was so scared I could see her hands shaking. The fear in her eyes told a complete story. Words were not necessary. Coffee leaned forward and picked up one of the marijuana blunts, lit it and started smoking. I was proud of Coffee. She held her ground, showed she was willing to play and didn't let peer pressure force her to play beyond her personal limits. I wanted to say 'touché Coffee. Don't take shit off nobody.' But Sweet Pea was a Royal Family original. A charter member of my family and Coffee wasn't. Sweet Pea's loyalty is not confused and never in question.

My phone rang, and it was Cheyanne Foxx. I answered on speaker as usual.

"Speak freak"

"Hey, just got settled in. I'm staying at the Venetian. How's everything?"

"Straight"

"How's everyone"

"Cool"

"Call you tomorrow, love you."

"Love you more"

"My God"

"My Goddess."

We both then hung up at the same time. Translation: How's everyone was her way of specifically asking about Coffee. Everyone is our code for outsiders. How's everything refers to financial business from the streets to the suites. We always end our calls with terms of endearment. 'The my god' comment is her way of saying there's no one I put above you. My goddess is my way of saying I put no one above you either. Sweet Pea snorted another line, picked up the platter, then sat in my lap as she placed the platter on hers.

"Hungry daddy?" Sweet Pea asked me.

    I then passed it to Sweet Pea and the rotation continued. Coffee grabbed up the last tequila shot and a lime sliver. We sat there for a half hour while loosely watching that Richard Pryor movie 'Another You'. Sweet Pea began kissing me. First, she started with my neck and began to work her way down to my chest. She rubbed my thighs then began performing fellatio on me while Coffee watched.
    This was just what the doctor ordered. With my head tipped back and my eyes closed I could hear moans coming from Coffee's section of the couch. The moans got louder and began to drown out the slurping sounds Sweet Pea was making.
    I began cuming in Sweet Pea's mouth, down her throat. She knows not to remove her mouth until every drop is drained. When I opened my eyes I was surprised to see that Coffee was masturbating as she watch us. Sweet Pea winked at me, then crawled over to Coffee and began performing cunnilingus on her.
    I lit the other blunt and started smoking as I watched Sweet Pea and Coffee. Coffee came so hard she squirted. Literally soaking my couch leaving it drenched. As Coffee collapsed on the couch, falling asleep, Sweet Pea and I shared the last blunt without Coffee.
    No words were spoken between us but as Sweet Pea and I met eyes an entire conversation took place. A conversation that required no words

and no facial expressions. We finished watching the movie then took a shower together. All three of us.

"Sweet Pea, what are you doing tonight?"

"The usual I may clean up the garage."

Translation: The usual, I may clean up the garage means working the track.

"If you need help with any heavy lifting hit me, I'll be close."

"You always are daddy."

Translation: I'm letting her know I'll be packing two guns with the heavy lifting comment. Coffee loved our language because whenever we speak it. She cuts a little smile. She has long since stopped trying to figure it out. We all began to get dressed. Sweet Pea couldn't help but notice that Coffee had very little to wear.

"Here Coffee, try this on." Sweet Pea generously suggested.

"Thank you"

Coffee embarrassingly responded. Sweet Pea left out first. She knew what she had to do. She was headed back to Hollywood. Sweet Pea was consistent and multitalented. She usually danced.

I was curious why she hasn't been at the club in a few days. I didn't bother to ask because her numbers hadn't dropped off. I knew that Cleopatra was dancing tonight then heading to the afterhours.

Glamour was out of town set up to work the NBA all-star weekend. Coffee had no idea what she was doing but she knew she'd be with me. When we left, Coffee wasn't her usual talkative self. The exposer had been fully exposed and had a look as if I was looking at her naked. Her eyes danced around my face but avoided my eyes directly.

As we drove I began to grope Coffee's thigh. She scooted over and opened her legs so my hand could fit. As I fondled her body, Coffee stared blankly out the window. As if she was in a trance. I went into the glove compartment to retrieve a pre-rolled marijuana blunt. I put it to my lips and without saying a word Coffee grabbed my cigarette lighter from the center console and lit my blunt.

We drove and smoked. I was headed to Gorilla Mike's house. Gorilla Mike was a Gorilla pimp who was a Piru blood gangbanger turned pimp. He wasn't too smart or graceful and had a stable of street walking crack whores. They worked Sepulveda Blvd in the valley. He owed me money.

When Gorilla Mike first got out of prison he had nothing. He had gone to prison for possession of crack cocaine for sales. I loaned him 10 grand to get back in the game. I didn't ask what the money was for. But I assumed it was for drugs. Instead he bought a use Lexus and started pimping.

Ten grand at 5% interest per week is 500 dollars a week. It's been 3 months. Each month around the first I collect 2 grand. Just in interest I had collected 6 grand from him and yet he still owes me 10 grand.

His last prison stint must have scared him out of the drug game. He wasn't smart enough to navigate successfully threw the pimp game. His lack of consistent success proved most profitable for me. He will never pimp up on 10 thousand dollars. Not with a stable of drug addicts. As far as I'm concerned, gorilla mike is a 500 dollar a week ho in my stable without even being aware of it.

We arrived at his apartment in Gardena. I didn't mind because it was on the way. Coffee got out the car with me before I could tell her to stay in the car.

She seemed to be in pocket and in character even though I knew she didn't know the intricate details of the part she was pretending to play. I appreciated her effort in doing to. It shows respect of fear. Too early to distinguish between the two. I knocked on the door and stood off to the side. Peep holes make me paranoid

"Hey man, ah Mickey...Mickey Royal...man what's up? I didn't expect you til tomorrow"

"I know Mike, that's why I'm here today." Expect the unexpected is one of my mantras.

"Are you gonna invite us in or are we gonna talk on the porch like Jehovah Witnesses?"

"Oh yeah my bad...come in, come in."

Mike was indeed a Gorilla Pimp and proud of it. He spends half his day beating up and intimidating women. I always establish dominance quickly and positioning for purpose of leverage negotiation with him. That's my way of reminding him I carry more weight in this game before he even begins to forget.

"Hey mick what you drinking? What can I get for you?"

"Money, mines…all of it"

"What you mean? All of it or what I pay every month?"

"That choice s totally up to you. I've been here 2 minutes already. Twice as long as I planned."

"Oh, okay"

Mike went to the back room. When he walked back into the room I had both hands in my jacket pockets. In my right was a .38 caliber revolver. Gorilla Mike wouldn't dare make a move against me. But I always go with my street survival instincts and whenever in any form of standoff and your opposition walks away. I know they're NOT coming back empty handed. He walked up front with a roll of money.

He kept sniffing and it wasn't flu season. His pupils were dilated. He was high as a kite. Tweaking apparently smoking meth. He was so busy concentrating on hooking his ho's on dope he must have gotten distracted and hooked himself. But that's an HP (His Problem) not an MP (My Problem).

"Here Mickey 2 grand it's all there."

"Of course it is"

I then tossed the roll to Coffee.

"Count it. Out loud."

She began just as I ordered. But then something funny happened. Coffee stopped counting at 1700. "Coffee please tell me you just came down with laryngitis."

"It's only 17 hundred here" said Coffee.

"Mick, I got 3 bitches on the track right now I'll have the rest tonight."

"No now you have one minute." Mike still sniffing screamed for one of his hos.

"Peaches where the fuck is the rest of the money bitch?!"

"I gave it to you Mike" Peaches answered in fear.

Then in typical Gorilla Mike fashion, Mike punched her in the jaw with a closed fist. Peaches fell to the floor then he kicked her in the stomach, jumped on her chest and began to strike her with the ferocity which could rival a UFC fighter. Coffee stood behind me with her hand covering her mouth.

"Oh my god" Coffee mumbled.

As I stood still and waited for an applicable pause in his display of force.

"Mike, unless she's a piñata full of money, I don't see how or where my money is supposed to come from."

"Naw Mickey, this bitch stuffing."

Stuffing is a term in the pimp game which means she's keeping a portion of profit and not reporting it. I knew this was a lie and all just a show designed to distract me and buy Mike more time.

The truth is Mike's crystal meth addiction has gotten the best of him and he smoked more than he made. Since the drug which he got on credit is now telling him what to do I decided to cut my losses and settle his account. I knew which dealers he more than likely owed and his life expectancy has been drastically reduced. I calmly tapped Mike on his back.

"Mike, get up. I like to look people in the eyes when I talk to them"

Mike did just as I ordered. Peaches saw her master obey me like a slave. Thus telling her to obey me also. Peaches survival instincts told her to fear the man the man she fears…fears. I told Mike and Peaches to sit on the couch.

"Mike, you still got that orange Cadillac escalade?

"I don't mean to correct you in front of yo bitch but its tangerine."

"My apologies, I mean tangerine" I replied sarcastically.

"Yea, I still have it, why?"

"Bring me the keys"

Gorilla Mike sat there motionless. He looked at Peaches and told her to go get his keys off of the dresser. Peaches stood up then I interrupted.

"Sit down Peaches. Mike, she doesn't owe me. You do. Mike go get the fucking keys." I said with more base in my voice.

My adrenaline was pumping by now. I didn't like being over Gorilla Mike's house. It stunk of drugs and unwashed clothes. I then walked over to the couch where Peaches and Mike were sitting and hit Mike in the side of the head with my .38 caliber handgun from my right pocket. Coffee screamed just as blood from the side of Mike's face hit the wall.

"Oh Jesus, shit just got real." Coffee said.

"Coffee go sit down," I said, pointing at the kitchen table.

Coffee swiftly moved to the kitchen and sat down.

"Damn man, alright. I'll get the keys." Never will I let a wounded angry animal out of my site.

"Peaches, now…Go get the keys." Peaches got up quickly."

"Yes sir." She responded to me.

"Mickey, you know I'm good for it. You and I have always been cool."

"Mike, we still are. This is just business."

Peaches came back with Mike's entire key ring. Mike's hands were shaking as he separated the keys.

"Mike, where's the pink slip?"

"In the glove compartment."

"Okay I'll sign your name. I just bought it from you for 10 grand. I'm keeping this 17 hundred as interest and our business is done. Consider your debt paid."

Peaches, packed a bag.

"You belong to me now. You have 3 minutes."

Peaches got up and did exactly as I had ordered. Mike was an addict now. He's Gorilla Pimping, selling crystal meth, and addicted to it. His money is short so I know he's getting product on consignment.

My street instincts tell me he won't be alive long enough to continue to pay the interest let alone the principle. So I closed the account. Peaches came from the back and Coffee, Peaches, and myself left together. I left Mick's Escalade parked where it was.

It's not going anywhere. Truth is, I didn't even want his hideous monstrosity of an SUV. But I had to leave with something. That brought Mike account to 77 hundred cash total and an SUV worth at least 15 grand. Not the way I wanted to end his account but a victory is a victory.

We all drove to the motel 6 by LAX. I booked Peaches a room for two nights. Motel 6 is located on Century Blvd which is a track. Since Peaches is a track star she knows what to do. We, Coffee, Peaches and myself, went to the room which was on the seventh floor.

"Peaches, what you got?"

"Mickey, you're holding everything I made. That 17 hundred."

"I'll be back to check on you. You belong to me now. I mean and that's it. When I return don't let me catch you empty handed. I mean you got a good look at Mike, right?"

"Don't worry Mickey, I understand"

Coffee and I left. Coffee couldn't wait to pick up that memo book as soon as we got back in the car. I noticed her hands were slightly shaking. We hit Century Blvd on our way to the Boom Boom Room. I hadn't decided what I was going to do with Peaches yet. Truthfully, she was one of the last things on my mind. When I was pistol whipping Mike I noticed Peaches had cracked a smile.

I knew then she would be coming with me. Besides, Mike would have taken his frustration out on Peaches when I left and probably beat her half to death. A woman beater is a coward. I had no intention on bringing Peaches into the Royal Family. I just may do a full court press sprint burnout. Cop and blow, get what you can then you go.

Coffee and I arrived at the Boom Boom Room on El Segundo and Avalon. I could see from the parking lot that the place was packed.

"Where are we gonna park?" Coffee asked.

"Valet" I swiftly answered.

122

"Oh, of course. I forgot who I was talking to."
"How?" I wittingly responded with a smile.

Then I winked my eye at Coffee as we exited the vehicle. I tipped the valet in advance. I always do. That my way of saying;

"Don't steal out of my car."

As soon as we walked up, the line started to split as we made our way through it. The outside security didn't know who I was apparently when he asked for identification. I pulled out my cell phone and called Lonzo from downstairs.

"Hey Lonzo, it's Mickey. Im out front." Less than a minute later lonzo comes down the stairs.

"Hey Mickey, glad you could make it doc" said Grandmaster Lonzo.

He escorted Coffee and I past the velvet rope upstairs. The joint was packed, wall to wall players. Beautiful women everywhere. A few ladies I recognized from the porn industry and new faces as well. Coffee and I were escorted to our reserved table in the VIP section.

"Wow, yours famous."

"I believe the word your looking for is infamous...unfortunately."

Coffee was mesmerized by the total flamboyancy of the evening affairs. She stayed safely close to me as I mingled amongst my peers. A woman approached me tapping me on the shoulder.

"Are you Mickey Royal?"

"All day every day."

"I'm Norma Stitz and I'm a huge fan of your work."

"To Which work are you referring?"

"Your books, I love your writing style."

"I'm honored and I know who you are."

Norma Stitz is in the Guinness Book of World Records for the world's largest natural breast size. Triple Z. When she walks into a room you can't help but notice. I can remember seeing her on the Jenny Jones show a long time ago.

"May I?" asked Coffee with her camera in her hand.

I smiled and moved closer to Norma. Well, as close as her breast would allow me to get. Coffee snapped the photo. This time she asked permission so she appears to be learning. We have strict unwritten rules and regulations which coincide with protocol and respect. In extreme cases, violations can be a matter of life and death...yours. I signaled

124

for Coffee to come to me using only my index finger. I wanted to know just how close attention she was paying to my slightest detail. Without hesitation, she swiftly complied.

"Yes Mickey?" she softly asked.

"Go back to our table. I'll be there in a second."

"Yes sir"

I wanted to discuss possible business ventures but tonight was neither the time nor place. In business as often in life, success is based on timing. It's much better to get a yes much later than a no right now.

So instead I made my way through the crowd over to my table. Just as I sat down a waitress came to our table with a bottle of champagne and 2 glasses.

"Our compliments" she said as she popped the bottle and began to pour.

"Ms. Coffee will you do the honors?"

"To what shall we toast?"

"To Mickey Royal, the most extraordinary gentleman I've ever known or known of."

"Cheers!" I responded as our glasses touched.

As Coffee and I were sipping champagne, enjoying the evening, the music and each other Lee Mack came over and I stood up to embrace him. Grandmaster Lonzo, the owner and host of the event came up and we were all standing and chatting. Just at that moment out of nowhere Coffee whips out her camera.

"Say cheese gentlemen."

I didn't mind her snapping that photo. I was starting to see that's who she was and what she does. Besides, it was a night for pictures. A lot of cameras were snapping. While we were standing around posing I received a text message;

'Wearing Mac make-up heading up the Nile.'

Translation: Make-up means Glamour. The Mac make-up refers to her having her total game face on. Heading up the Nile as in the Nile river in Egypt. That means she's on her way to Cleopatra's. Cleopatra must have called her to her swingers/voyeur's VIP party.

I texted back;

'Are you swimming or sailing?'

'Swimming'

Translation: Sailing asks is she directing? Swimming asks is she participating? I'm assuming one of Cleo's Hollywood clients saw a picture of Glamour in her photo album titled 'The Menu' and personally requested her. Cleo's clients pay 1000 for starters. With this recent news I was most pleased.

"Coffee, it is now time we bid them adieu."

Coffee stood up, grabbed both of our coats and followed behind me. As we got to the bottom of the stairs I paused to allow Coffee to catch up. Coffee draped my coat on my shoulders as the valet pulled up with my car. We headed back to Gardena to claim my prize. Gorilla Mike was more gangbanger than pimp. Still cool, calm and collected as always, I was ready for any and everything. It could be nothing or there could be a bunch of Compton Piru gangsters waiting to put holes in my body that my body wasn't born with. One on one,,
Mike was no match for me at all. In my glove compartment, I kept a .38 revolver. In the lining of the driver's seat, professionally hidden was my Winchester sawed-off double barrel shotgun. It has two triggers and only has two shots. In my past experience, I've only needed one.
I looked over at Coffee as she realized where we were going and said;

"Expect the unexpected."

Since my car is recognizable I parked halfway down the opposite of the block

"Do you have a driver's license Coffee?"

"Yes"

We got out of the car and retrieved my Winchester sawed off. I got 5 shells from the trunk then loaded it with two shells leaving three in my pocket. The right pockets in my coats all have holes in them. I cut holes in them so I can wear my trademark trench coats with my hands literally on the concealed weapon of choice. A little trick I picked up in my youth as a 13year old curb serving crack dealer. Coffee was no longer her usual nervous self. She was officially terrified beyond the capacity of rational thought. Paying close attention to my every detailed instruction with life threatening intensity. I had my revolver in the small of my back. We were ready.
"Follow me" I ordered Coffee and she obeyed.

I walked directly in the middle of the street as to draw out any hiding potential adversary. I handed Coffee the keys as I stood guard on the corner. Coffee quickly cranked the car and drove around the block as I walked back to my car. I looked everywhere but there was no sign of Mike. When Coffee came back around the corner she was driving a lot faster than she should have been.
I could tell something was wrong but had no idea what. She pulls up right next to me and rolled down the tinted passenger side window.

"Mickey, in the back! Check the back-row seats"
Coffee screamed.

I opened the rear-passenger door to find the slightly
decomposed corpse of Gorilla Mike. I couldn't tell
if he had been shot or stabbed, hell maybe both.
This is the reason why I've never accepted dope on
consignment when I was in that business as a youth.
I learned early from the mistakes of my
predecessors at the time. Rule number one, you
don't inhale the retail.

"Coffee he can't hurt you. He's dead, I Mean really
dead. Follow me and watch your speed."

I said that to Coffee while purposely exposing my
shotgun just in case she decided to take a detour to a
police station. In this lifestyle, we settle all disputes
disagreements and cases out of court.
     She drove behind me as I drove to the
marina. I knew no one was there and she would feel
safe there. So far since she's been with me that was
her most familiar setting.
     When we pulled up Coffee parked on the
street. Hopping out fast and hopped right in the car
with me. I parked my car in the underground
parking space then and I headed to the elevators. As
soon as we got inside I took the keys from here.

"Stay here, don't answer the front door for anyone.
I'll be back son."

"okay"

I drove back to Century Blvd in the Escalade where Peaches was working. I pulled into the parking lot and parked in the back behind the dumpster. I didn't get out of the Escalade. I was aware of the cameras. I climbed to the back where Mike was. I took off his gold chain with a Gorilla medallion, his pinky ring and close to 600 dollars from his pockets. I opened the back and pushed him out behind the trash dumpster. I crawled back to the driver's seat left swiftly and hit the 405 Freeway.

I knew when they found his body they'd review the tape. They will see the license plate and go to Mikes House. I had just until daybreak to decided what to do with this orange, oh excuse me tangerine escalade. I chose motel 6 as the dumping site to send a subliminal message to Peaches. Even though the car was technically mines I had a signed pink slip with my name on it.

Since I hadn't turned the paperwork in to the DMV, this is one prize I won't be collecting. As we say in dominoes; 'All money ain't good money.' I took the 105 Freeway till it ran out and abandoned the truck at the beach.

I knew there were no cameras there. I got out the SUV and began my journey back on foot. I couldn't use my cellphone to call for a ride. I didn't know Peaches. I didn't know anything about her but she was with Mike when I took possession of the vehicle. So she could place me with the vehicle as in ownership. If I make a call, the cell phone tower could place me at the location of the vehicle. Just to play it safe I removed the battery as I walked.
Blank (Pictures)

Lee Mack, Grandmaster Lonzo and Mickey Royal.

Norma Stitz and Mickey Royal

Chapter 4
Tuesday March 18th

I walked back to the city of El Segundo where there was a phone booth in front of a 7-11. I called Cheyanne Foxx, the one person I knew I could trust. She was recently back from a Vegas business trip filming her comeback video shoot. She came immediately to pick me up.

"How was Vegas?" I asked her.

"This was the first movie I directed so I think I did well. I had a great teacher." Cheyanne said as she rubbed my thigh and smiled.

"How's Coffee. Is she getting on your nerves yet?"

"No, she's been good company."

"Have you fucked her yet?"

I laughed and said;

"No, have you?"

We both enjoyed a good laugh. Cheyanne began to tell me about a book she was writing. I was listening but all the while I had Peaches on my mind.

"I'm sorry it took so long to pick you up Mickey but the cops had century all blocked off, where too?"

"The marina"

I was so glad she happened to mention that about Century Blvd. That took time off my schedule so I had to make a battlefield decision. When we pulled up I told her to park her car in my space when I pull out. I have unfinished business elsewhere.

"Coffee is upstairs, keep her company."

Cheyanne had her own key. I headed back to the Motel 6 and went up to Peaches room.

"Hey mickey, guess what? They just found…oh"

Peaches stopped in mid-sentence when she saw me wearing Gorilla Mike's trademark gorilla chain around my neck.

"You were saying?"

"Nothing, nothing at all Mickey, I mean daddy."

"I don't ask, when you see me break bread immediately."

She had close to 500 dollars and I'm sure she broke bread with every cent. By exposing his chain to her the implication was clear and obvious. Unknown forces rule more absolute than the truth itself. She had the fear of God in her eyes as her eyes were focused on me.

"I own you 100%"

"I hope so" she replied.

Peaches began to kiss me and dropped to her knees to perform oral sex on me in a prayer type posture. As I stood there with my hands on my hips looking down at the top of her head I recapped the Gorilla Mike account. I loaned him 10 grand 4 months ago. I collect 2 grand a month for 3 months and 1,700 yesterday. That's 7,700 plus 600 from his dead pockets which is 8300.

8,300 plus 500 from Peaches comes to 8,800. I had to give up the Escalade but I took his experienced

500 dollar a night bottom bitch. She will soon be a 1000 a day Lady of Leisure. As she finished I told her to come with me. Gorilla Mike had beat her so much that her soul was damaged and her spirit was destroyed. She was rough around the edges but I've sculpted masterpieces with worse lumps of clay.

She grabbed her one suitcase and we checked out. I drove her to Hollywood where Sweet Pea was staying. We walked upstairs so I could introduce them.

"Sweet Pea this is Peaches, Peaches this is Sweet Pea."

"She'll be staying in your guest room. Get her indoctrinated then assimilated. Get her some pictures post the m in the LA Xpress and LA Weekly publications and get her in-call started."

"Okay"

I left. I kept it short and to the point. Sweet Pea was most like Peaches out of my wives. There personalities were similar and I knew they'd hit it off. I didn't know exactly who killed Gorilla Mike and I didn't care. I knew it was one of three suppliers. The only three who would have given him credit. As far as Peaches knew, 'The man who terrorized her is no more at the hands of the man she now calls Daddy.' I can expect 15-25Gs consistently per month form her.

So all things considered it was a good day.
I hated having to give up that Escalade. When I got
back to the marina I parked on the street. I knew if
Coffee was going to blab about tonight's events
then Cheyanne Foxx's ears were as safe as it came.
I had no idea what to expect when I walked through
those double doors. I live my mantra 'Expect the
unexpected.'

So I walked in. I didn't see anyone. I walked
in my room to find Coffee in nothing but one of my
shirts and Cheyanne in nothing but one of my shirts.
Coffee was with me when we found Gorilla Mike
dead so to wear his chain any longer would be a
moot point. I took off his chain and rings and placed
them on the bedroom dresser.

I'm not into jewelry, not anymore. When I
was younger I did the gold chain thing to death. At
this point in my life I prefer a more sophisticated
contemporary look. It comes with age, with
maturity. My father always told me to 'Dress for the
job you want, not the job you have.' It's about
elevation and expansion.

I decided to unwind just a little so I took
both ladies to a bar across town called 'The Cork.'
On Adams between La Brea and Crenshaw. It was
one of my familiar hangouts when I use to frequent
the neighborhood. I could tell Coffee felt right at
home with Cheyanne and myself as we ordered
drink after drink. Since alcohol makes me sleepy I
decided to high-tell-it back to the marina while my
eyes were still open and I felt as though I could
drive.

I couldn't tell if Coffee had discussed tonight's events with Cheyanne and personally I didn't care. When I looked directly at both of these ladies I felt all three of us had only one thing on our minds. Needless to say, they laid me down, undressed me and an earth-shattering ménage a trois ensued. This was just what the doctor ordered. But still cool calm and collectively in control.

Tantalizing to the taste buds Cheyanne Foxx is. Having absorbed her essence til our souls became one. It is I who authored the notes of her symphony she so beautifully conducts. Watching from behind the curtain in awe as she stands as a living testament to my perversion. Much like the Mythical Medusa turning the mightiest men to stone with one glance.

Men stand frozen in their tracks after a mere glimpse of the 6'1" Golden Goddess Cheyanne Foxx. With mouths agape, tongues unroll like red carpets serving as runways when she struts. Men compete to be her slave as she kneels before me as her master. Her life serves as my lifeline. The very flesh I feed upon embodies every elemental aspect of my existence. Unable to unlock her most thunderous inhibitions without my presence makes my participation mandatory.

The next morning, I woke up first to find both Coffee and Cheyanne still asleep. I emptied my safe and took the cash to my accountant as I did every few days. I don't like having cash in my spots. I spend more time in my cars than I do at anyone spot. I take the cash to my accountant who's also a tax attorney. She then cuts me a check made

out for our LLC, minus her 8%. I then deposit that
check and it starts over again.

I drove through the hood and gave Gorilla
Mike's jewelry to the first bum who asked me for
spare change. I didn't want to keep it, bad karma.
Besides it's evidence. Just then I got a text from
Sweet Pea which read; 'Fruit is ripe, making a pie
tonight.' Translation: Peaches is ready and we're
working tonight. When I returned to the marina
Cheyanne was gone but Coffee was still there.

"Don't you have to be going to school? Spring
break is over in a few days."

"Mickey, I don't have anywhere to live. Can I live
here just til I get back on my feet?"

"No. How can you get back on your feet when you
have no employment?"

I knew what Coffee wanted. She just wasn't ready
to say goodbye to my world and hello to hers.

"Mickey, I can cook, clean, answer phones, run
errands and you won't even know I'm here. But I
have nowhere to live at the moment."

I was hoping Coffee didn't think she could
threesome her way into my head, heart, or home.

"Did you tell Cheyanne about what happened last
night?"

"I don't know what you're talking about. Nothing happened last night so there was nothing tell." I knew she was referring to Gorilla Mike.

"Where's your memo book?"

Coffee went into my bedroom to retrieve her memo book. She read her notes out loud to me. It contained names, addresses and incriminating facts...evidence. She walked over to the stove to set the memo book on fire. I watched with puzzled anticipation and then I stopped her and explained that with a little editing and re-arranging it would be okay.

"I never lived until I met you. I need you in my life for the rest of it. I will do whatever it takes to be one of your wives. Mickey, I love you."

I knew that was the adrenaline of this week's events talking or was it her logical mind making a conscious irreversible decision. Nevertheless, Coffee was a grown woman.

"Careful, careful, careful Coffee. You enter this world nothing will ever be as it was in your life."

"You promise? Don't threaten me with a good time." She wittingly responded.

"No one comes before Cheyanne. You do understand that?"

"I know she special to you. All I'm asking is for a chance to be special to you too."

This hit me from left field. Coffee would be perfect for adult films. I didn't want her to jump right into escorting. But we're the Royal Family.

Each one of my wives are well trained and experienced veterans. I had been with them a long time. Coffee handled herself well under pressure and Cheyanne trusted her. But there was still one question I had to have the answer to.

"Coffee why can't you live with Cheyanne if yours so close like family?"

"Mickey, Cheyanne owns two cats. I'm severely allergic to cats."

At that moment, I exhaled. As a family to accept a new family member first a lady must choose and Coffee has done that. Then the entire family sits down to takes vote through secret ballot. All of the votes have to be unanimous. Peaches hasn't even been voted on yet. Whether she makes it to the round table for vote depends on Sweet Pea's report. That takes a few weeks.

"You may stay here for now. We'll see, see if you learn. Have you ever considered dancing or doing adult films?"

"Can't say that I have."

"Start"

"yes sir"

Coffee answered as she switched back to the bedroom in classic exaggerated Mae west fashion. As she passed by me I lovingly slapped her on the butt. I couldn't tell what perfume she was wearing but she smelled good.

I knew she had no true idea of what life she was entering, or did she? The main thing I liked about Coffee was that she was smart. I wondered how she would look at school through not so innocent eyes. There's a saying, 'The Pimp Game, once you enter, you're never the same.'

I went into the bedroom where Coffee was draped across my bed. Her body twisted seductively in the satin sheets. She was still caught in a web of ecstasy. Where the fork in the road meets at the intersection of fantasy and reality. I've lived my entire life there. My once youthful fantasies became my adult realities.

In a world where my life plays out as one long short continuous day. A place or state of mind, a state of being where time is altered, development is arrested and night and day are but mere shadows of the abyss. A place where sleep is an unaffordable liability. Thus, forcing me to live out my dreams.

A world that is cloaked in broad daylight and is as visible as the New York skyline at night. A world where you hold the key to freedom but choose to remain locked in. A virtual maze of deception with forced perspective realities. The Shadow World.

A world of angels and demons, ghouls and goblins, predators and prey masquerading as homo sapiens. Disguised cleverly in silk, satin and mink. I exist therefore I am and I'm as old as the scriptures that foretold my arrival.

In the book of Genesis, I am a sinister snake. In the book of Revelations, I am a solidified serpent. My power grows daily. Feeding from the 'tree of knowledge' fertilized by the uncontrollable vices of man. His weakness is my strength. His insecurity is my source of power. I bathe in the sea of iniquity.

And yet I forever thirst. Fueled by the wants of many, the needs of few and the desires of all. For I dwell inside of you. Feed me with your lust, your greed, your fears and delusions of grandeur and I will appear.

For only I can cure you from the self-inflicted infection that I gave you. Continue to worship me as you always have. I reside in your soul consciously guiding your actions while deeply rooted in your subconscious. As I look out of the bedroom window I see the sun staring me in the face. Shamefully I shy away from my loyalty I pledge to the guiding light of the moon. My nocturnal source of power. State of mind preceding state of being. Genesis chapter 6, verse 4, verifies my official birth. Ecclesiastes chapter 1, verse 18, my predestined fate.

Humility is modesty apologizing for its mediocracy. Arrogance is loud, confidence is quiet and power is silent. The Izm is ever present and its author's ever-living. From the 'three of knowledge' I feed. From the river of wisdom, I drink. From the air of understanding, I breath.

Total supremacy flows through my veins. Possessing a panoramic view of the present. Possessing a peripheral view of the past while maintaining tunnel vision for the future which is now. All have bowed before me undocumented because I've never noticed. Time ticks one way and waits for no man. Power exceeding the paranormal.

My venomous fangs drip at the site of untouched forbidden fruit. Hand delivered to me by the one I love. Offering a piece of a special part of you as a sacrifice. A lifetime of dedication and devotion. Never-ending flattery tickling my ego ever so gently. For I am you, and you are mines.

Coffee became instantly relaxed in my presence. The marathon threesome with her and Cheyanne Foxx released deep hidden desires within her psyche. Over the next few days I planned to explore the very limits of her inhibitions til they are repressed no more. Adding yet another soul to my purgatory of paradise. This sin-filled oasis constructed by the hedonistic hypocrisy that claims it as it's nemesis. My neck is strong enough to support the crown but not flexible enough to support two faces. There is no conflict within me.

Cheyanne knows me better than anyone. Coffee was hand-delivered to me. I didn't know if Coffee was fully aware that she will no longer be riding everywhere with me. The job of a leader, a coach, is to assign his players to the best position suitable for the benefit of the team.

"Coffee, are you almost finished your project?"

"You still want me to go to school?"

"I'm not here to change your life, rather to enhance it. To add an exclamation-point where a question mark once stood."

"I love the way you speak. You talk funny."

"Funny? And you've yet to crack a smile."

"That's what I mean. I'm so glad I know you."

"You don't, but you will." I said to Coffee as she silently paused to process the possibilities of the worst possible scenario.

"I'm not afraid."

I rubbed her lovingly to reinforce the security she expressed that she feels in my presence.

"No, I don't believe you are afraid. And you have no reason to be."

"Well I'm afraid of the other wives not liking me."

"With that I have no control. I don't use my influence to sway the votes."

"I know your vote is yes huh daddy?"

I turned her body around slowly into doggy-style. I decided to have a quickie before heading out. After having sex, Coffee got up to take a shower.

"What should I do?"

"Oh you're just ready huh?"

"When do they vote?"

"In due time Coffee. Enough with the questions."

"Okay sir."

Coffee seemed to be eager not to make a mistake. I still needed her to be close to me for a while. She was with me the entire time during the Gorilla Mike incident. She handled herself well but trust has never been one of my stronger qualities. I've turned boys into men, men into little girls and little girls into women, and women into men. I have personally contributed to man's inhumanity to man. I have orchestrated the evil that men do.

I've stared the evil in the face and lived to tell about it. But I never told. I'm the subject of orgasmic fantasies, sweet dreams and horrific nightmares within the same sleepless nights. Coffee I didn't yet full trust so I wanted her close to me for a while before getting her feet wet. She may think she's ready to swim in the life but I've seen better than her drown. In my younger days, I would have had her erased just with the mere thought of her one day tying me to a crime that carried life in prison.

The clock I feed have never bit my hand because of my style of feeding. Coffee was no different. A car is a car. Each make and model may drive differently but the general mechanics are the same. Fueled by the same mechanisms. Such is the human mind, body, and soul.

"Let's go shopping."

Coffee quickly grabbed her purse and we left. We went to Cheyanne's in Hollywood. I was hungry and I wanted to stop at Pink's for a hot dog but the line was too long so we kept going. Along the way I said and did what I had to do to keep Coffee talking. I didn't want to pick her brain. I didn't wish to dig. That would be easy but guarded. I wanted her to get comfortable and chatty to see if she volunteered any information about the subject of Gorilla Mike.

She was with me while I interacted with peers of my fraternity in The Shadow and Underworld. She didn't bring up any names nor mention recent meetings or events. There was no longer a memo book. I didn't want Coffee to receive an F on her report.

I needed to figure something out which would protect the identities and activities of myself, my constituents and the Royal Family. But at the same time salvaging her work. I make sure my wives have something to fall back on.

When you enter this life your exit plan is as important as the very rules and regulations.

"Coffee, what's the name of your report?"

"Well I don't know yet but the subject is Urban Enterprises. I truly believe I was destined to be with you. I get a good vibe from you too."

As much as we talked, the subject of Mike never came up. Still though, loyalty is measured in time and activities. This was seen in my eyes as a test that she seemed to be passing. Doing the right thing according to the rules and regulations is like flexing a muscle. Eventually you relax, get sloppy, make a fatal mistake. The right thing has to be so saturated in your philosophy of everyday life that it becomes instinct. With hesitation or processing.

This is not what we do. This is who we are and how we live. The jungle can be a frightening dangerous place, but not to a lion. To a lion the jungle is his domain. The world in which he rules from the top of the food chain. It was time to complete Coffee's transformation from prey to predator. We pulled up at Cheyanne's. I called Cheyanne from downstairs.

"Hey love!"

"Hey lover!"

"Downstairs now"

"On my way."

In about five minutes Cheyanne came downstairs. I told Cheyanne to take Coffee shopping. I gave Cheyanne 1,000 dollars to assist Coffee in her make over and new wardrobe. With them gone it would give me time to make my rounds collecting, check on Peaches then get the wives assembled for a vote.

As I drove to Sweet Pea's, Peaches was on my mind. She was not Royal Family material but she was a seasoned veteran. She feared Gorilla Mike like a God and in her mind, I killed him to take control of her. Even though nothing could be further from the truth, the truth is relative. Backed by and supported by belief and or a system of beliefs Gorilla Mike was accustomed to. She was trained by and kept in line by the fear of bodily harm.

I learned early in life that loyalty is based in love. Obedience is based in fear. Fears are challenged, naturally tested by the human spirit. Love is comfortable, secure and once proven is welcomed by that same human spirit. I would run inside a burning house to save someone I loved. Just as most humans would. I would not run inside a burning house to kill someone I hated. I would not run into a burning house to escape someone I feared. There is only one human element that is strong enough to inspire the human spirit enough to override human nature... That element is love.

My family runs on love, equality, and trust. These are key elements that must be marinated to maturity to produce loyalty. My concern was that Peaches may need too much psychological construction to repair decades of emotional destruction.

The debate was within myself. Should I keep and attempt to transform Peaches? Or should I let her go on her way once I've collect 10 grand to properly balance the closed Gorilla Mike account? Should I erase Peaches before if and or when she verbally places me with Mike's murder? Her future, her very life rests in my opinion of her and the direction in which she is capable of going. Sweet Pea's evaluation of her will be more important than she could ever imagine.

I went to Sweet Pea's. I usually stopped by there after leaving Cheyanne's spot since they were both in Hollywood. Close in proximity as far as miles. Worlds apart as far as personalities go. I didn't call before I came. I did have to. I have the keys. When I came in I was pleased to see two gentlemen sitting on the couch. Sweet Pea came from out the hallway bedroom to take on of the gentlemen in the room. I didn't say a word to the men. Both were nervous, wondering who's the mystery man in black with his own key.

I stood by the door still...silent. I could hear Peaches moaning in the back room. The headboard was slamming into the wall. It sounds disturbing to the ears of squares. To me it sounds like a cash register. Sweet Pea looked me in the eyes, winked, said nothing, then took one of the gentlemen to the room. Before they went inside I heard the gentlemen ask her;

"Who's that guy?"

"What guy is that?"

"The one dressed in all black"

"He's not a who, he's a what" then the door closed.

That type of blind loyalty can only come from such blind loyalty. I give as I receive. Until I can plant that seed in Peaches I'm forced to rely on and reinforce fear until the seed of loyalty can blossom into maturity.

Peaches finally came out from the back bedroom with a gentleman walking in front of her. He left without making eye contact. Sweet Pea had apparently given Peaches a bit of a crash course on the Royal Family protocol. Because Peaches didn't say a word to me either. She winked her eye, smiled, then aggressively snatched up the other gentlemen and took him to the backroom. A woman like Peaches can appreciate not having to walk to the track. Risking her life dealing with 50 dollar tricks with bad attitudes.

Word had gotten around that Gorilla Mike's main lady was with Mickey Royal now and Gorilla Mike was dead. Mike was once a big-time dope dealer who let his lust for women cloud his greater judgement. Then he entered The Pimp Game thinking his success would be transferable from game to game.

There's big differences between The Underworld and the Shadow World. A well trained experienced ho can turn an inexperience pimp upside down. Mike started using the drugs he once sold. His life then began a downward spiral until he was in a Gardena apartment with 3 scared to death crack whores. I didn't know Peaches drug of choice yet but if she was with Mike then she was on something.

Sweet Pea came out a few seconds before Peaches. Both escorting gentleman to door. Now I spoke;

"How life?"

"It's fine" answered Sweet Pea.

Translation: how is she working out? Sweet Pea handed me 2,300 dollars.

"For one night?"

"From both of us" Sweet Pea answered.

I was pleased that Peaches had no problem handing over money to Sweet Pea. Sweet Pea was happy to have direct authority over someone. At that moment, I made Peaches Sweet Pea's responsibility. I knew Sweet Pea really wasn't into powder cocaine or weed.

I supplied marijuana to my wives. We have an indoor marijuana grow located in the marina in the second bedroom. We have 10 plants. Half of the plants are for the Royal Family. The other half I exchange for blow for my wives who choose to partake or sell to VIP regulars only. The barter system keeps the family profits untouched by vices. I exchange cash for nothing. I don't pay for party favors. The Izm is my master.

I left to go see Glamour. She danced in Van Nuys at a gentlemen's club in the day. She was also a model and often worked well with Charlotte. Glamour was often requested by Charlotte Web's high-profile clients. She lived up to her name. Glamour was glamourous. Her theme song was of course 'Glamourous Life' by Sheila E. Glamour didn't smoke, drink, or do any drugs. She was a nymphomaniac and a vegetarian.

I stopped by Cheyanne's first to see if they had made it back yet. I noticed Cheyanne and Coffee were still gone so I kept going. I texted Cheyanne; 'Drop off groceries on the beach when you finish shopping' 'I love you'

Translation: Bring Coffee to the marina spot when the two of you are done. Cheyanne always texted I love. That meant okay. The track, conventions, in-call, out-call, pornography, events, strip clubs, swinger parties, voyeur shows, long tall cons, websites you name it. I've done it. It's all about activity. Mix it up, stir up the pot and run the whole gamut.

When it came to my wives, I loved each and every one of them. Some I love like a sister, some like an aunt, some like a daughter. One doesn't exploit family. One protects and respect family. I didn't want Coffee involved in porn. She was in college and when she finishes with her career as an adult entertainer there will be no trace of it. I knew Coffee and Peaches were from different worlds to be dealt with differently. But the two ladies will be forever connected through the Mike incident.

The time was coming when Cheyanne could no longer hold Coffee's hand. I wanted to see how well she could ride her bike without training wheels. I got to the strip club in Van Nuys. I walked in and Glamour was serving drinks. She liked to dance in the daytime because there were less dancers there.

The location of the club was in the heart of downtown Van Nuys, and near LAVC college. She took full advantage of their active happy hour. I came in and took a seat in the corner. It took nearly 10 minutes for Glamour to see me. She came over immediately. I ordered a vodka that I had no intentions of drinking. I was a ruse to have her stand by me.

"Mickey let me give you a lap dance." She took me over to the corner of the club where it was dark.

I knew she must have had something to tell me. So I sat and she began to dance on my lap.

"Mickey, you see the dude over my shoulder in the yellow shirt. He's trying to Gorilla Pimp on me. He twisted my arm last night and took my money. When I came out the house this morning he was parked outside. Then he followed me here."

As glamour spoke my rage grew. Glamour was a model, full of finesse. She wasn't streetwise like Peaches.

"He followed you? What kind of car does he drive?"

"He's in the black Range Rover in the parking lot."

"Stay here, do exactly as I say. Pay close attention to each golden detail. When do you hit the stage again?"

"When I want."

"Get back on stage and dance till I return."

I got up and left. I drove down the street to Home Depot. I purchased a black wire for .29 cents. I drove right back to the club but parked down the street from the club. I got my screwdriver out of the trunk. I went to the back of the club and saw the black Range Rover. I unscrewed his left rear break light. I connected one end of the wire around the brake-light. I put the other end of his gas tank. I walked to the street, looked back, and saw that the wire was not visible by the naked eye. The wire blended right into the paint.

I walked back into the club where Glamour was dancing just like I said. I motioned for her with my eyes for another lap dance. I sat at the bar. I noticed that Mr. man was seated right in front of the stage. She came over to the corner and began giving me a lap dance.

"Glamour after you finish dancing get dressed. I'm parked at the end of the block. I want you to walk out of the front door and head up the street on foot. Go bring me your keys. I'm gonna pick you up in your car."

Glamour had been with me long enough not to ask questions. Her eye brows raised, then frowned as she agreed. She did just as I ordered. All of the family members had copies of each other's car and house keys. I went to the parking lot and hopped in Glamour's black Corvette. I didn't bother to adjust the seat. I just cranked up and left.

As I left I saw Glamour walking fast down the street as I drove up the block. Just as expected Mr. Man followed right behind her. She had a half a block head start so he ran to his Range Rover led by his egotistical rage.

He cranked the engine and nothing happened as soon as he stepped on the brake it sent an electric charge from the light, through the wire into the gas tank. If the wire wasn't long enough nothing would happen. I didn't measure the wire. Just as I began to wonder then I heard the explosion. It was so strong it shattered car windows down the street. I pulled up on Glamour.
I could tell she heard and felt the explosion. The entire neighborhood did.

She got into the car then we drove back to retrieve my car. That's when Glamour saw the smoke and heard sirens in the near off distance. "What the fuck?!"

"Expect the unexpected. He won't be bothering you anymore. How many clubs do you dance at?" "Mickey, you ended that question with a preposition and Two. I also dance in Gardena."

"Dance there from now on."

My wives were well acquainted with my methods of operation. I got into my car and she and I drove off in opposite directions. My rule is; 'I never second guess nor question my wives.' She could have been lying about Mr. Man but family first. Did I go too far? Was that a bit extreme? These ladies risk their lives, reputations, and being disowned by family members for the good of their new family. Should my risk be any different? As a coach, a commander, I will never send someone into a situation that I myself wouldn't venture into first. When your family knows beyond a shadow of a doubt that you will risk your life, life imprisonment or take a life at the drop of a hat par their request. It makes it easier for them to do so for you. I'm too seasoned to play games with Mr. Man. Glamour is too valuable to me not to come to her rescue. The way to have people willing to do anything for you is to be ready, willing, and able to do anything for them. Van Nuys is hot now and closed off for work. I wanted Glamour to steer clear of that club.

I'm sure she'll tell the owner the in light of recent events she no longer feels safe working there. As I ran into bumper to bumper traffic on the 101 Freeway I received a text from Cleopatra;

'Headed to Miami. Big fish on the line.'
Translation: I'm being flown to Miami by a member of the Miami Dolphins. Big money involved.

'Order a pizza if you get hungry.'

'Copy that.'

Translation: If you need me or run into trouble call me and I'll come and do whatever I have to do.

Since traffic was at a standstill I pulled off of the freeway and went to the Sherman Oaks mall. I got my gym bag out of the trunk and decided to go to the 24 Hour Fitness. Not to workout, I just wanted to relax in the steam room for a while. I sat and just chilled to gather my thoughts.

I was enjoying the sweet sound of silence. I did my usual 20 minutes then it was on to the hot tub. I truly appreciate the fact that its co-ed. I was meditating, thinking hard about absolutely nothing. I had my head tipped back and my eyes closed. I could hear people getting into and out of the tub. I was quietly eavesdropping on the hot tub gossip and conversations around me.

In life, one must enjoy simple pleasures. Listening to the mundane tales momentarily

provided a temporary escape from the maze of complications of my lifestyle. When I opened my eyes, I was face to face with two apparent stereotypical soccer moms. Neither wearing a wedding ring. When my eyes were closed it seemed to amplify the power of my hearing.
Because I heard every word when my eyes were shut. But when I opened them their perfect diction was reduced to muffled murmurs.

So I tipped my head back and once again I could clearly make out the blonde telling the red head how sexy that black guy was. I assumed they were talking about me seeing how I was the only guy in the hot tub who fit that description. I personally wasn't feeling particularly handsome. I desperately needed a shave and a haircut. I hadn't made time in recent days to schedule a barber shop appointment.

The entire Coffee project threw off my entire routine. First, I was her tour guide, then lover, then roommate, and now soon to be main man. Life possesses no pattern so I expect the unexpected, always. They seemed to be more comfortable speaking about me with my eyes closed so I closed them again, then tipped my head back.

The blonde was telling her red headed friend that she was going to approach me before she left. I took that as a que to make myself approachable. So I got out of the hot tub and announced myself.

"I guess I'll get going, ladies have wonderful evening."

They both smiled and waved with a hint of a giggle. I know that giggle. When I got dressed and left the men's locker room both ladies were standing at the end of the hallway. We walked out together as if we arrived together with me in the middle. I guided the ladies to the Cheesecake Factory (Which is in the same shopping center) for drinks where I could effectively work my magic. I turned up the Izm slightly in order to move the night along. I had Cheyanne and Coffee waiting in the marina for me.

"Ladies will you please excuse me? I must make a call."

"Hurry back" said the blonde.

I went into the men's room to text Cheyanne Foxx. I want to accelerate the Coffee process.

'Crystal ball?'

'White words'

'Print and run hot drink'

'You got it'

Translation: Crystal balls means, where are you? White words mean Hollywood referring to the words written on the Hollywood sign mountain. Print and run hot drink means take pictures of Coffee (hot drink) Print and run means place (in-call ad in the LA Weekly and LA Express so we can see how Coffee can handle herself). The marina is a good location only if you have regulars. Hollywood is centrally located for an upstart.

I came back from the restroom and both ladies had men speaking to them. I noticed the blonde rolled her eyes while one of the men were speaking. I walked over, just close enough to make eye contact with the blonde. I motioned for her to come to me. The blonde tapped the redhead and they came running toward me like two emancipated slaves.

"What about the bill?" I asked.

"Those guys paid it" said the redhead as three of us laughed and left.

When we got to the parking lot the ladies asked me to follow them. I followed them to a ranch-styled house in the Valley Village. It belonged to the red head.

"What do you do?" The redhead asked me

"About what? If you want a more detailed answer you'll have to finish the question." I replied.

The blonde asked, "What do you do for a living?"

"I manage adult entertainers."

"Really? I am an adult entertainer."

"I'm not surprised. A lot of women in the Valley are."

A conversation ensued and at the climax of our discussion I pulled the redhead to me and began to kiss and undress her.

I recognized the blonde as the alpha female. That's why I went for the redhead, the beta female. One's aggressive. And the other passive aggressive. By using the power of suggestion threw the beta female I ensured success with the alpha. Within the minutes we were evolved in one of the most exciting ménage a trois I've ever participated in.

I've been having threesomes since the age of 14. After a couple of hours, it was time for me to leave. The blonde asked me to join her in the bathtub for a little one on one time. Extra innings if you will.

"I didn't catch your name" the blonde said,

"I never threw it."

As we made love in the bubble bath the redhead snapped pictures. Then she snapped a few more pictures as the blonde and I went for round three. As I got dressed I noticed the redhead becoming increasingly shy and the blonde were seriously interested in acting in adult films. All she was speaking about was porn and Adult Entertainment. She definitely knew her way around a man's body.

"My name is Mickey Royal"

"I'm Joclyn Stone."

I never got the redhead's name nor saw her again. I left headed towards Hollywood. I called Cheyanne and told her to pack enough clothes for a few weeks. Since Glamour is no longer dancing in Van Nuys which was her bread and butter she would have to increase her in-call action. I then made Glamour aware that I wanted her to work out of Cheyanne's Hollywood spot for a few weeks. Glamour would be dead meat with two seasoned barracudas like Peaches and Sweet Pea.

By the time I reached Cheyanne's, Glamour was already upstairs with Coffee. Coffee has been under my wing or Cheyanne's wing since she chose. It was time to see if she could fly. An assessment test if you will. I took Cheyanne with me and Glamour and Coffee stayed behind. Plus in light of today's events in Van Nuys with Mr. Man it was a good idea for Glamour to be out of the 818 area for a while.

I still wish there was some way I could have kept Mike's Escalade. But getting rid of it was the smarter choice. Before we left the area, we stopped by Sweet Pea's. Cheyanne went upstairs and collected for me. She came downstairs with 2,300 dollars. I sent her back upstairs with 1000 for Sweet Pea to take Peaches shopping.

She wore cheap bargain basement bullshit. Totally non-representative of the Royal Family standards and reputation. They seemed to be averaging 1,000 a day each. Cleopatra's long-con style of working a trick brought in five figures minimum.

But the bigger the fish, the longer it takes to reel them in. Different fish swim in different waters. Each body of water must be sailed and navigated differently. Each type of fish requires different type of bait. I had personally trained each and every one of my wives. My core Royal Family members. I hadn't added new ones in a while.

My wives are so well trained and completely immersed in the Izm that they possess the ability to train others.
Giving the forbidden fruit, the eye-opening mind expanding dark art of mysticism is alive. Flowing like blood through veins and arteries in one celestial body.

Cheyanne and I headed to the marina. Jocelyn Stone was texting me. I handed Cheyanne my phone and dictated to her what to text. I texted her the address of my Hawthorne spot. I had a place where I conducted most of my adult film business. I wanted her on film as soon as possible. At this location, I kept my lights and cameras permanently set up. I told her to meet me there tomorrow night. That would give me enough time to round up a male counterpart for her to work with.

When Cheyanne and I got to the marina she expressed that she was hungry. We went to the Cheesecake Factory which was my second time today. Same restaurant, different location. I desperately needed a haircut and shave. I could only hope I didn't look as tired as I felt.

Pimping Ain't Easy

While waiting to be seated Cheyanne and I began kissing passionately like two newlywed teenagers. Getting lost in love losing track of time. Totally forgetting we were in the center of a crowd of many. A woman who appeared to be with a pack of female co-workers asked us;

"How long have you two been together?"

"When did time begin?" Answered and asked Cheyanne?

"At the big bang" I responded.

Cheyanne looked at the woman said,

"Since the big bang"

then I said;

"Theoretically"

We were always turned on and fully turned up. We sat and ordered. I ordered the chicken salad and she ordered shrimp scampi.

"Cheyanne, I can't kiss you now. You ordered shrimp. You know about my allergies.

"My bad daddy. In the future, I will be more conscience of your shellfish ways."

"Okay baby…Hey I caught that."

"Finally, I threw is so long ago."

Our eyes met then we ordered drinks.

"Moscato for the lady and Mojito for myself." I said to the waitress.

Even though our conversation was epic I still was struggling to stay awake. It wasn't a reflection on her, I was just that exhausted. I excused myself to go to the restroom.

"I have to go power my nose, excuse me."

I went to the stall and did two lines of Peruvian blow then quickly returned to my table.

"Daddy, you left a little power on your nose."

I wiped my nose and we enjoyed a laugh. I figured that a little jolt would wake me up. Our drinks came first so now I could properly come down without dire consequences.

We discussed her upcoming book and film projects. She was going to start producing and directing a whole slew of soft core adult films aimed at promoting swinging and couples therapy through healthy sexual practices.

Cheyanne's proposal would take the Royal Family mainstream and out of the shadows. I discussed with her about producing my films. Lessons on the Izm taught by a true master who knows. Not these clowns and imposters who flood

YouTube. Helping squares go from simp to pimp and in some cases wimp to pimp.

I texted hooks from the table. He was an established adult film actor. He would be perfect in the scene with her. I hadn't directed an adult film in weeks. This would knock the cobwebs off the old camera. Also revitalize a once lucrative revenue stream to coincide with the family's new direction.

That meant more money for everyone unilaterally across the board. Every family has a patriarch and a matriarch. A mom and dad. A king and queen. The Royal Family has one kind Mickey Royal, one queen Cheyanne Foxx, and many princesses. I refer to them as wives and princesses. As you label, treatment follows.

I don't have a stable, I have a family and we serve and protect the union. Our strength is rooted in unity and our loyalty is pledged to the collective. I once heard three may keep a secret if two are dead. My mother (a former Black Panther) once told me 'No one can hear what you don't say.'

Glamour trust the family with her life but she knows not to discuss the Mr. Man incident when with them. It never happened. We don't gossip even amongst each other. Neither of us could finish our meals. Maybe our eyes were bigger than our stomachs. We both got doggie-bags to go. We were just blocks away from the marina spot so we took our time driving there. The conversation was healthy but I still needed sleep.

I honestly could barely keep my eyes open. Cheyanne had no idea that we almost wrecked twice. I actually fell asleep behind the wheel.

When we walked in I went to the bedroom to prepare for a shower. She and I shared a shower.

We both put on our pajamas and rolled a few marijuana blunts then sat up watching Three's Company re-runs on cable. I decided to attempt to rescue Coffee's project by an extensive Q&A. I explained to Cheyanne all that it involved while we smoked. Cheyanne's a professional columnist, novelist, aside from a model and actress. The majority of the time I spent with Coffee was to lay a foundation for her research paper. Cheyanne is well versed in the Izm therefore she can skip that stage and dive into it. I wanted Cheyanne to help her with her paper.

While we were still smoking I felt comfortable to see that she had already started working on her laptop. I don't remember finishing the blunt. I couldn't. I passed it one last time then drifted off to la la land. Like Santa's elves Cheyanne worked through the night while I slept. She added some insert pages for Coffee's paper.

Pimping Ain't Easy

Adult film legend Joclyn Stone

Mickey Royal and Joclyn Stone

P

169

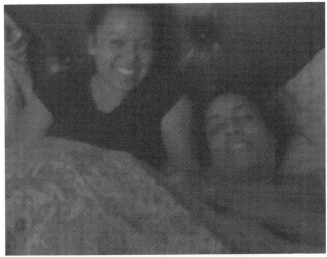

Coffee and Cheyanne Foxx out one night with Mickey Royal (pictured below). The next morning (pictured above).

Chapter 5
Wednesday, March 19th

When I woke up the next morning she was gone. Cheyanne left me a note on the door which read 'Glamour called while you were sleep. She said that it's a thumb's up so far. Be back after I leave the gym muah smooches.'

After I read her note I went to sit on the couch and fell asleep again. This time only for a few hours. I awoke with the sounds of my phone ringing. It was Hooks hitting me back confirming 8pm for the Joclyn Stone shoot. I wrote a note for Cheyanne letting her know that I'll be in Hawthorne. I rolled three blunts, put them in my cigarette holder then left.

On my way to Hawthorne I got a call from adult film Hall of Fame legend Janet Jacme. I hadn't seen her in a while. I had a few hours to kill so I had her meet me in Northridge. Her schedule was hectic, so we agreed to meet in the city of Carson at 10pm. I got to Hawthorne and made sure everything was in place.

Joclyn had gotten an early start. Then she called to say she was stuck on the 405 freeway. She sounded excited and enthusiastic over the phone. I sat and patiently waited on the cast of actors while working on my laptop on yet another book.

I never really checked on Charlotte Web. She is self-governed, and she checks in periodically. Some work well without people over their shoulders. Others work well with constant supervision requiring a lot more attention.

Charlotte was the first of the two. I couldn't call Cleopatra because she was wrapped in an imaginary relationship with a naïve young football player. That's what we refer to as deep sea fishing.

There always a risk of losing your bait because of the length of time it takes to reel in the fish. She's deep undercover no pun intended. She'll surface or contact me when it's safe. If she's in a so-called relationship, then a phone call or text from another man could blow her cover thus compromising the entire mission. Not to mention a total waste of irredeemable invested time.

Joclyn arrived first. I had my lights set up and ready to go when she arrived.
We started of course with pretty girl shots. Pretty girl shots are pictures in lingerie or panty and bra.

Then it's on to the nudes. I use this location for nothing but XXX photos and film shoots. The refrigerator is there merely as a background prop. Just for when we start the scenes in the kitchen. She was a natural. She took to posing like a fish to water. The camera loved her. When hooks arrived, we set up in the kitchen. The shoot went off without a snag. I paid them as adult entertainers and we all left at the same time.

I had already secured a buyer for the scene in Chatsworth in the morning. It was quickly approaching 10pm. I had to meet up with Janet Jacme in Carson. At the last minute, she called me and changed the plans. She wanted me to picker her up. She didn't feel like driving. As I hit the freeway heading to the valley I got a call from Joclyn. She spoke candidly about how much she enjoyed meeting and working with me.

She wanted me to put her at the top of my cast list. She said that her availability was open and she was eager for film and webcam work. This was cool. One can never have too many revenue streams. I pulled up where Miss Jacme was staying. She was only in town for a week. I texted her to let her know I was outside waiting.

She came right out. Since we were already in the valley we just headed up the 101 freeway to Extended Stay Hotel. As soon as she and I walked in we began to catch up on old times. We started to kiss then the inevitable. One of the greatest compliments I've ever received during sex came from her that night. I was categorized and filed in my mental rolodex as a true milestone. I had her nude laying face down eating her out from the back.

I just love the way a woman's ass cheeks feel against my eyelids. As she was approaching her second orgasm I began to toss her salad in several rhythms. Then I stiffened my tongue as hard as I could. I stuck it out as far as I could until I felt discomfort under my tongue. I began to anally plunge her with my tongue. When I thrusted in deep I would twirl the end of it. The same technique I use to tie a knot in a cherry stem. When I would bring it out I would counterclockwise lick and suck her asshole. Often scraping my teeth ever so gently. This continued all night.

When I came up for air she looked back at me. Rose up and said,

"Ooh you're nasty."

I wanted to make sure I heard her correctly so I leaned in closer and asked,

"What did you say?"

She got close enough where our lips touched and said.

"I said you're nasty."

Coming from her it was one of the greatest compliments I'd ever received. Then she kissed me and laid back down on her stomach. I began thrusting again and again inside of her. The sounds of her sinful screams in my ear echoing off of the acoustically challenged walls. The louder she was the more I grew inside of her. Humping, Pumping, back bending, back breaking fingernail raking down my back. Her tear-stained face wrinkling, tears mixing with sweat trickling unto my body burning hot dripping on orgasmically soaked sheets.

To her inner passion I've found no equal. Instead of taking her sexuality into left field I decided to dig deeper into centerfield. Thus turning down the kink and turning up the intensity. Burrowing deep inside of her. She was tight and surprisingly warm. Her vagina felt as if she was giving my entire body a hug. Mere mortals could never understand the complexity of reaching Janet Jacme's orgasm. Her sexual level is on a peak matching only my own that we mesh and melt into an erotic orb. The expressions on her face told my eyes her side of the story. We had sex for over an hour.

As we got dressed we shared a blunt which seemed to make her very sleepy. On the ride home to drop her off she fell asleep. I would like to believe that the multiple orgasms put her to sleep and not the marijuana. At least that's the way I will remember it. I've always revered Janet Jacme as an entertainer. She's one of the nicest women I've ever met. Just a joy to be around.

I headed to the marina. It would make more sense for me to spend the night at the room because I'm coming right back this way tomorrow morning. But I knew Cheyanne was waiting on me. And knowing her she probably cooked. I rolled down both driver side and passenger windows so that cool night air would keep me awake.

As the wind hit my face and still in a marijuana haze the sounds of the CD Zapp's Greatest Hits booming loud through my speakers. Where was I? On the 405 Freeway headed south just about to merge onto the 90 Freeway to head back to the marina. In reality, I was in another dimension all together. An altered sense of space and time. A place where you're in the middle of a dream with your eyes wide open. You try to wake up but can't because you already are.

I never ask permission in life. The odds are 50/50 on a no and even greater on a maybe. It is easier to have an apology accepted than to be granted permission, so I do or do not. The practice of analyzing the process to elevate anxiety is rooted in fear. And fear doesn't live here. It exists not in the Shadow World. Our world's cast is made up of predators, prey, and scavengers.

I pulled up and went upstairs. I went inside to find Cheyanne standing in blue lingerie with Adult film star/legend Kira. Kira was a legend in the game. Kira was wearing black lingerie'. I hadn't seen Kira in a while. Apparently, Cheyanne had decided to call her over to shoot a solo masturbation scene.

Cheyanne had always commented on Kira's oral skills. I didn't know what to expect but the unexpected. I saw two beautiful women but no camera. Kira initiated the action with me first then the two of us devoured Cheyanne. Explosive to say the least.

Time stopping electricity, primal instincts collide only to assimilate into earth shattering euphoria. They say if you want something done right do it yourself. I say if you want something done right, hire professionals. For an insatiable sexual appetite such as mines I'm forced by my own desires into the exclusive realm of erotic professionals. Kira had a pair of the most beautiful breast I'd ever seen.

Dear sweet amateurs, for the faint of heart need not attempt the sexual feats that professionals perform so easily. As I was pleasuring both women simultaneously I gazed upon Coffee's awestruck face. I could taste her dripping inner-core from across the room. I left Kira and Cheyanne both orgasmically exhausted. Afterglow assisted by Jack Herrera top notch sativa cannabis and tequila shots with lime slices.

As much as I enjoyed participating I chose to opt out of round 3 and made a few calls while Cheyanne and Kira displayed a sensual soliloquy in 69 for my enjoyment. Asking, ordering, demanding and ultimately begging for my involvement. Coffee sat in the chair, taking pictures and occasionally masturbating during our power hour. I felt guilty for keeping her up so late by herself. I walked into the bedroom only to find Glamour who was snoring already. I crawled into bed with her and passed out.

Adult film legend Janet Jacme and Mickey Royal at the motel.

Adult film star Kira, Mickey Royal and Cheyanne
Foxx at the hotel.

Glamour

Chapter 6
Thursday, March 20th

Just a few hours later my phone rang. I had
just drifted off into a deep coma-like sleep when the
sound of the telephone opened my eyes. It rang four
times before I gathered the where all's to answers. It
was Cleopatra. She was calling to inform me that
she had landed at LAX international airport. I got
dressed and headed out. Apparently, the phone call
had not awakened Ms. Foxx.

The sun was just coming up. You could
smell the dew and frost in the air. It reminded me of
when my mother use to take me to school as a child.
That's the last time I can remember being up so
early. My nights usually end at daybreak. When I
arrived at LAX, I appreciated the fact that Cleopatra
was outside curbside waiting. The traffic was hectic
as always.

She hoped in the car and gave me the biggest kiss. I have to admit I missed her. Cleo's game was subtle but strong.

"Are you hungry?"

"No daddy. I flew first class. I ate on the plane. We had salmon and some kind of pasta dish."

Cleo had only 1,500 dollars on her. I took 1,000 of it then waited for her to justify her back and forth flights for the past three months. She knows my patience level when it comes to the family finances.

"He's flying out here tomorrow with an investment check for 75,000. I told him I needed 100 grand to put the down payment on a 50 unit building in Houston, Tx"

"What's the catch?" I asked because I've learned from experience that there always a catch lurking.

"He wants to marry me."

"Are you gonna marry him?"

"Mickey I'm already married." Answered Cleopatra as she rubbed my ring finger.

Cleo could sense my sudden change in mood as an eerie silence fell between us. Knowing me as along as she has she continued before I could make a battlefield decision.

"I got this daddy, I promise."

There was slight concern in my mind mainly because I detected doubt in her voice. I knew how she felt. Her reputation as a hustler was on the line. A three-month project without baring fruit could cause a family vote. The wives could end up voting her out.

    Cleo had been with me for many years but Royal Family constitution stands as is and I can't show favoritism. Cleo does not need to be made aware of this fact. She is well aware of it.

"He's flying in tomorrow with the check and a ring. I may need your protection. Will you be available?"

I didn't dignify that question with a response. I knew why she asked it though. It was a weapon. A passive aggressive comment designed to put me on the defensive. She felt disrespected in my line of questioning. Dually noted, so the silence returned.

"We've added a few fresh faces since your departure."

"Really? How can you hold a vote without me present!?" Cleopatra asked with a hint of anger in her voice.

"There have been no elections held yet. We were patiently waiting on you."

Cleo smiled after that comment and the eerie silence lifted. It was still early and I hadn't had any sleep. Cleo reached into my glove compartment for my cigarette case full of pre-rolled blunts and lit one. Cleo wasn't much for weed or any drug for that matter. But I guess she was nervous about tomorrow. Her rep was on the line and she knew it.

I took her to the Hollywood Hills swingers house. This mini mansion was part of Cleo's game. It's partially the reason she is able to pull pro athletes and high-profile clients. Her game was somewhat similar to Charlotte Web's. Even though they both primarily dealt with high profile clients, Charlotte was known in her circle as a swing party promoter and fetish fantasy provider. Her exclusive clientele call her with the most outlandish requests and she makes sure that fantasy gets fulfilled at any and all cost. Kind of a modern-day Mr Roarke from the old Fantasy Island tv show. But its wham bam with discretion and confidentiality.

Cleopatra specialized in the 'love for lease' game. There are many paved roads that lead to the same destination. Since we all possess different skills and abilities, chances are that most of us will be traveling on our own particular highway. Cleo specialize in the road less tailed by. Her game was sinister, cold, calculating and highly effective.

Cleo's main residence was the Hollywood Hills location. Such a location is necessary as bait for her to reel in such big fish. Or in this case a big Dolphin. I dropped her off and told her that Charlotte's last swingers party left it a mess. If her Miami Dolphin is flying in town tomorrow she had her work cut out for her. I left and hit the 101 North headed to Chatsworth to sell that Joclyn Stone and Hooks scene. I figured I might as well since I'm wide awake and already in Hollywood. I smoked another pre-rolled marijuana blunt and popped in my Superfly soundtrack CD. I was feeling no particular way while driving to Freddie's dead.

I went to Gentleman's video. This was the place I sold a majority of my xxx scenes. It was owned by a 64-year-old Italian from New York named Michael Esposito. He had served as a mentor to me in the adult film industry business. He had been around since the beginning. He was old school blood and guts. He was from Harlem not Hollywood.

When I got there, we shot the shit for a while in his office. Just small talk. Then he cut me a check in my company name and I left. He had another meeting scheduled and I needed to check Coffee and collect from Charlotte. So after 20 minutes there, I left.

Sherman Oaks was on the way back to Hollywood so I went to Charlotte Web's first. She had a car in the driveway I couldn't recognize so I parked across the street and waited. Hours went by so I leaned my seat back as far as it could go and took a cat nap.

Apparently, I was sleepier than I thought because when I woke up the sun was setting. It was at least 5 o'clock. The car was no longer in the driveway so I rang the doorbell four quick times to alert her it was me then entered with my key as always.

Charlotte was happy to see me to say the least. She pulled me into her master bedroom and we made love. It was quite passionate, very oral and patiently sensual. That was her style, the slow hand, the easy touch. It last for hours. I was well rested from my nap. I felt strong and alert.

Cheyanne had been begging me to take a vacation for years. She constantly accuses me of burning the candle at both ends. I do not measure right and wrong, time and space the same as most. The unseen ever-present owner of the pure and living Izm flows through me, guides me. It is the un natural pathway to true freedom and unlimited power.

As I laid across Charlotte's king-sized bed and white satin sheets she went into her closet safe. She tossed a brown paper bag on my stomach. She mounted me and kissed me ever so gently then whispered in my ear.

"I love you. I love you so fucking much it scares me"

She licked my ear then got up to shower. The bag seemed light for Charlotte but the game, the life us is up and down. Besides even Charlotte's low days are above the average. I got dressed and left while Charlotte was in the shower. I drove down to Hollywood.

I texted Sweet Pea and Glamour the same message. 'OMW2U'

Translation: On my way to you.

Traffic by now was heavy. So I got off on Ventura
Blvd and took the streets to Hollywood. I collected
from Sweet Girl and Peaches then went to Glamour
and Coffee who were posted at Cheyanne's condo.

"We had a problem this morning daddy"

"Such as?"

"Coffee leaves every morning. She said you told
her to stay in school. I told her that daddy wants his
money. She just works after school."

    I detected quite a bit of jealousy in
Glamour's voice. She handed me two separate
stacks. She handed me 1,300 then she said,

"Only 500 is from her" Glamour knows separating
is a no no.

"She was right Glam I specifically told her to stay
in school. Glam, school's out next month just relax.
Remember how new she is. I know she's not on
your level. Complete her, don't compete with her.
Okay?,,,Okay?"

"Okay, I'm sorry. I know better, forgive me."

"There's nothing to forgive."

I kissed her then went straight to the Royal Family's
accountant. I got quarterly profit and loss sheet then
exchanged cash for multiple checks.

I then made my routine deposits. I headed back to
the marina spot and placed a call to Cleopatra;

"Light bulb tonight. I'll screw it in your kitchen."

Translation: I've got an idea that we must speak
about in person. When I got back Cheyanne Foxx
met me at the door naked. We started kissing and
making our way to the bedroom but never made it. I
got as far as the kitchen floor. I never realized how
cold my kitchen floor was until my naked body was
pressed against it.

Once finished I went and took a shower and
changed clothes. Cheyanne was headed to
Hawthorne. She was going to shoot two scenes for
her new movie. She said it would only take a few
hours but I knew she would be all night. One of the
scenes was an orgy scene.

Cheyanne and I left out together. She got in
her car and I got in mines. I went back to
Hollywood and requested Peaches for this particular
assignment. She was with a client so I waited
downstairs. I stood by my car and got sucked into a
conversation with a meth head about government
conspiracies and 9/11.

Peaches came downstairs in one of her new
outfits. She wasn't as pretty as the rest of my wives
but she had a killer body. She made up for any short
comings with work ethic. It's not about beauty, it's
about duty. And she's dutiful. I was beyond happy
to see Peaches come down those stairs. Not because
I missed her but because the meth head's
conversation went from insightfully intelligent to

pattern-less and paranoid. I thought my ears were going to melt off.

We left headed to Cleo's in the hills. We took the street. When we arrived, Cleo wasn't expecting Peaches. But she knows if she's with me then she pre-approved. Originally I had Coffee in mind but this plot required a pro. You can't learn to box during a championship fight.

For an assignment such as this I would normally use Cheyanne. But Cheyanne Foxx can be a bit intimidating. She stands 6'1" barefoot 6'5"in heels, she's ½ Brazilian and ½ Greek. I needed this to be believable. Besides, Peaches is really not Royal Family material but she's earning well and holding her own. If she handles this right she's a shoe in for a unanimous vote.

We got to Cleopatra's and Peaches was mesmerized by the size of Cleo's house. The house is in the Royal Family LLCs name but Cleo primarily occupies it. Sometimes a few of the wives appeared to be jealous but the house is conducive to her style and level of game. Peaches never imagined the family was on this level. Especially when she noticed the classic convertible Rolls Royce Corniche in traditional canary yellow.

We walked in and Cleo had fried chicken and potato salad on the kitchen table. We discussed the plan after dinner then I drove back to the marina alone. I left Peaches with Cleo to get acquainted and to let the plan marinate. Also, Sweet Pea is comfortable working and living alone. She's done an impeccable job with grooming Peaches on our family's rules and regulations.

She seemed to understand our proper protocol.

I then went to see Charlotte Web. I informed her of her new itinerary. Charlotte was the final piece in the delectably evil plot but the information I provided to her was only what concerned her. The Shadow World rotates on an axis of whispers which revolves around secrets. Charlotte went to work immediately, right in front of me even before I left.

When I left I called adult film hall of fame legend Jeannie Pepper. I knew she lived close by so I invited her to join me for a workout at the 24-hour fitness. I figured since I was in Sherman Oaks I might as well get a workout in.

I went by her house to pick her up. I always kept a gym bag in my trunk with gym clothes. I also kept my bowling ball and shoes in my trunk. When I went to pick her up she came to my car to put her gym bag in my trunk. When she saw my bowling ball bag she expressed that she'd rather go bowling. So she ran back in to change clothes. I had already changed into and was dressed in my gym clothes.

On the way to bowling she asked if we could go by Big Lots first. She wanted to pick up a few items. We stopped in and did a little shopping then went bowling. I bowled one game with her then we decided to hit the hotel. I really didn't have time because I had preparations to make. But this was world famous Jeannie Pepper so I made time.

At the hotel she gave me a full body massage with baby oil. It was quite nice. My shoulder was sore from bowling. The sore shoulder isn't the reason I lost. She was just a better player, that time. After my massage, I returned the favor.

I gave her a full body massage with the baby oil. Before I got her too comfortable I flipped her on her back and began to perform oral sex on her. She reciprocated and we fucked fast and hard. She had a pair of the most beautiful breasts I've ever seen. I enjoyed sucking them, tasting them, caressing them, cuming all over them.

The ultimate MILF with timeless beauty. Her breast are truly in a class by themselves. I can only compare the taste of her juices to an overly ripe peach, nectar of the gods. So soft, so succulent and still so satisfying. Appetite and thirst quenched immediately transforming me temporarily into gluten.

I lost track of time with her, but thoroughly enjoyed myself. Housekeeping just knocked on the door and came in. If she had come in 10 minutes earlier she would have gotten a shocking surprise. Since she was standing there staring I handed her a camera and said,

"Why don't you take a picture? It will last longer."

The maid did just that. She took our picture. Then I asked the maid are there any more uniforms in the stock room? I gave her a hundred dollars for a 20-dollar used uniform. She ran to the stock room. About 5 minutes later she brought me the uniform. Then Jeannie and I left. She was puzzled. Why would I want this? But she didn't ask. It didn't concern her. I dropped her off back at home. Then I drove back to the marina to await several calls and or text messages.

Cheyanne still hadn't come back from shooting yet. She texted me and said she needed me to meet her at the Extended Stay hotel. That's where she was shooting this last scene. Before I left I poured myself a glass of cranberry juice. Charlotte placed some calls to her sports agent friend in Dallas Texas.

The word was that Cleo's new fiancé was flying in tomorrow night and would be staying at the Bonaventure Hotel. I didn't know if Cleo knew it or not.

I went online and booked a room in Bonaventure Hotel. I grabbed my .357 magnum chrome with the 8-inch barrel. Then I drove downtown to check in. I went upstairs to the room. I put the 100-dollar maid's uniform in the top drawer then I left. I drove back to pick up Peaches. It had to be near 1:00 am by now. Because of the time I called instead of just using my key. After two failed attempts Charlotte answers,

"Yes baby"

"I'm outside"

"Then please come…in" said Charlotte Web in her sultry southern drawl.

I came in to find Peaches had fallen asleep. This was the first day she hasn't worked. I guess it just caught up with her. I drove her to the Bonaventure Hotel. She was half asleep but that didn't bother me. She just needed a good night's sleep. Sweet Pea's pace is brutal and nonstop. I'm sure Peaches had been doing everything she could to prove herself.

As soon as she hit the sheets she was out cold. Glamour, Coffee and Sweet Pea were where they were supposed to be doing what they were supposed to be doing.
While Peaches slept I text Cleopatra

"20? Touchdown?"

"Nina sunrise"

Translation: 20 refers to location. Touchdown means money in bank. Nina refers to the term 'Nina Ross' which is street vernacular for a 9mm pistol. Sunrise means am so the wire transfer will clear.

We had roughly up to 24 hours til confirmation drop. I had to pair off Peaches with Sweet Pea. Sweet Pea is the only one of my wives street enough to begin Peaches transition.
The transition is first then the transformation.
Peaches had grown up in foster homes.

She was with a highly abusive Gorilla Pimp who took out his failures on her physically. Looking at her naked took a strong stomach. As she slept in the nude next to me I stared at her body. She had bite marks, belt lash marks, scars where stiches had been, and cigar burns. Threw all of that I saw a beautiful creature.

Everyone who had come into contact with her had taken advantage of her. Her entire life had been spent immersed in fear. I rescued her from her fear (Gorilla Mike) only to replace it with her terror (Mickey Royal). In her mind, there was nothing and no one scarier than Mike. And Peaches believed I killed Mike. Jesus said, 'As a man thinketh so is he.' Since Peaches is only fluent in the language of fear. I must become that fear by increasing that fear in order to then guide to become responsive to positive reinforcement.

Then and only then will she be truly ready to wed Sir Mickey Royal and become a wife. An official member of the Royal Family. Cheyanne and I will discuss it later. I figured now was as good a chance as any to grab 40 winks. Or at least 30. As she laid there, asleep on top of the covers, lightly snoring I couldn't dare wake her. I popped Seroquel and went to sleep. I accidently overslept.

Cleopatra

Adult film legend Jeannie Pepper and Mickey
Royal at the motel.

Chapter 7
Friday, March 21

I woke up at 11am. I saw I had missed several calls. Peaches was awake and sitting up watching television. Much like an abused woman flinches when a hand comes near her face. Peaches suffered from PTSD. She was several damaged, her spirit destroyed. Peaches wasn't born this way. She was made this way through years of systematic abuse. Peaches noticed I was visibly agitate and she reacted as if her life was in danger.

"Mickey mick mick. Daddy, oh, um, sir, I didn't know if I should wake you, answer the phone, or let you sleep."

I could have told her it was okay to ease her fears. But I frowned at her and said nothing.

I texted Cleopatra;

'?'

She texted back;

'Touchdown with extra point'

That meant the money has cleared. I needed to be sure so I texted back,

'!'

Exclamation point was code for are you positive? I then told Peaches to 'suit up'. She hopped up and put on the maid's uniform as I instructed. I texted Cleo;

'?'

She didn't text back. That means stand by. We waited almost an hour. I waited impatiently but didn't express it. Then I got a text;

'447!"

Which meant room 447 now. I gave Peaches the nod. She went to the room. As she walked for in the hallway she passed Charlotte Web in the hallway and bumped into Peaches slipped the key into Peaches' pocket. Peaches walked in and saw a passed out Miami Dolphin.

She undressed and took pictures with him
with his private parts in her mouth. Cleo walked in
and screamed at the top of her lungs. Peaches was
caught in the act as Mr Miami dolphin slowly woke
up. Cleo had laced his fruit punch with a ton of
Benadryl's. Miami Dolphin had a hard time
standing he was groggy.

"The wedding is off!"

She threw her wedding ring at him then she
ran out of the room. Peaches ran out when Cleo
screamed. She hit the stairway. She raced down the
stairs and pulled the fire alarm on the wall. Time
was a factor. As Peaches ran down the stairs he
undressed. When she got to the bottom of the stairs
she was met by Charlotte Web with a black trench
coat. Charlotte wrapped her up and they drove
away.
Mr. Miami chased Cleo down the hall
apologizing. When Cleo got to the lobby she saw
firefighters and hotel security,

"Help me! He's crazy!"

Security tackled Miami and detained him for
authorities. The press was on the scene in a half
hour. And Cleo was nowhere to be found. I calmly
walked out the front door of the hotel. Now the hard
part. Everyone scattered. Now it's about re
grouping. Cleo didn't drive so I had no idea where
she was. She ran out on foot. Hundreds of
possibilities ran through my mind.

Before I could let my paranoia get the best of me I got a text,
'Sixth!'
I rolled up to the sixth street and there she was. She hopped in the back seat and laid down in the backseat. She told me how everything went down.

"I wish you still had that 40,000-dollar wedding ring."

"You mean this ring?"

She had thrown a cheap imitation cubic zirconium. He wired 150,000 dollars to an escrow account with both their names on it .The wire transfer we were waiting on was her 125,000 dollar wire to our corporate account. She left 25 grand. I don't know. Maybe she felt sorry for him. I didn't ask.

I dropped Cleo off at the marina spot then went to pick up Coffee and we drove to the Hollywood Hills mini mansion. I told her we're married if anyone asks. We waited for hours. Hours turned into days. I felt like a cop on a stake out. Then finally after four days the knock came. Mr Miami showed up with cops. I answered the door. Mr Miami pushed his way in.

"Where's Sheila?"

"Who?"

"She lives here"

"You're trespassing only myself and my girlfriend live here"
"Soon to be wife" said Coffee.

The police had to physically restrain Miami after attacking us both. We sat calmly as the police searched the house. Pictures of Cleo were gone. Her clothes were gone. Miami ran to the garage to lift the door. He screamed to the cops that there was a rolls Royce in the garage. The cops told me to open the garage. I opened it and even to my surprise the garage was empty.

Cleo was good. Really good. Miami walked away puzzled. He isn't aware of the missing money yet. He was crying about his lost love. Ironic the historical Cleopatra was murdered by a poisonous snake. Cleo is a poisonous snake with a murderous bite. We waited an hour after they left then we left. I drove Coffee back to Glamour at the marina spot. I walked in and was met by Peaches, Cleopatra, Cheyanne Foxx, and Charlotte Web.

"Ladies we got 125 grand and a 40-thousand-dollar ring."

"The ring is mines. I earned it. I'm keeping it" said Cleo with authority.

The ladies looked at me. I paused and stared Cleopatra in the eyes. She stared right back. There was a long silent pause then I spoke,
"The rings yours."

"Thank you Mickey."

"Likewise"

Cleo usually took a week off after one of her long cons. I can only assume that it takes a lot out of her. She was emotionally drained. I texted Sweet Pea;

'All hands-on deck.'

Translation: Drop everything and come to the marina. Sweet Pea came alone. I wanted them here until Miami left town tomorrow. I went to bed with Cheyanne and Cleopatra. Coffee slept with Glamour on my pull-out couch. Sweet Pea slept on a pallet she made on the floor and so did Charlotte. And Peaches slept on my inflatable twin bed I kept in the closet. It resembled a sweet sixteen slumber party.

In the morning when we woke up everyone was properly dressed in their Royal Family uniforms, which is sexy pajamas or comfortable lingerie. I myself included. As ladies of leisure and myself as a gentleman of leisure, it was just second nature. As soon as everyone was awake, I sent Peaches and Coffee into my bedroom so the family could vote.

The hat is passed around for a silent secret ballot. I state pros and cons of both potential members but I myself don't vote. I just conduct the election. The ballots were in. I called Coffee and

Peaches out of the bedroom I had Cleo drop Coffee
and Peaches back off in Hollywood.

The ladies got dressed and did as I
instructed. Cleo took Coffee to Cheyanne's and
Peaches to Sweet Pea's. I myself along with
Cheyanne Foxx, Glamour, and Charlotte got
dressed and piled up in the Cady and left about two
hours after them.

We were headed to Hollywood to deliver the
election results. When we arrived in Hollywood we
stopped at Sweet Pea's first. We all went upstairs
and made it official. Charlotte had an engraved
Royal Family wedding band

"Peaches step forward" said Charlotte.

"Do you accept Mickey Royal as your sir and
Cheyanne Foxx and your madam?"

"I do"

"Then with this ring we wed, we bond. May this
never be broken. Welcome to the family."

It was something about the word family that struck
a nerve with Peaches. She was in tears. She kissed
Cheyanne then myself. Then she came downstairs
with us. Sweet Pea and Peaches stayed. She said she
wanted to clean up and go to work. We came to
Cheyanne's but I went upstairs with Cheyanne's
only.

In Cheyanne's living room sat Coffee, Cleo,
Cheyanne, and myself. I spoke,

"The votes are in. The votes must be
unanimous…they weren.t There was one no vote.
I'm sorry."

Coffee burst into tears then directed her rant at
Cheyanne.

"I'm a grown ass woman. I want this, I need this.
I'm not a little baby anymore."

Cleopatra interrupted Coffee in mid moment.
Arguably before she could say something shed later
regret.

"The one no vote came from me, not Cheyanne."

"The no vote was mines" said Cleopatra.

"You, why? You don't even know me. I was
working with Glamour. I only really met you once."

"When I met you, I knew you looked familiar. I
couldn't remember where I had seen you. Then I
remembered. It was in the mirror, twelve years
ago."

Cleo's eyes had swell up with tears but not one drop
rolled down her beautiful face. She walked over to
Coffee and gave her the ring Miami had given her.

"This ring is worth 40 grand. Take it and start over.
When you get older you'll understand my decision."

Coffee ran to me. For one last plea. I stopped her in her tracks.

"My wives have spoken. Elections final."

"Where am I gonna go from here?" asked Coffee.

Cleo looked back and said,

"Go to school"

As Cheyanne, Cleo, and myself walked out of the door Coffee, who was still visibly in somewhat shock said,

"Mickey, I love you!"

Cleo turned around and said,

"One day a man will put a ring like that on your finger and you'll love him...I did"

Just then a single tear trickled down Cleo's face and disappeared into the carpet. Coffee, who was still upset, yelled again,

"Mickey, I would have loved you for the rest of your life. You know you can't turn a ho into a housewife!"

That was when I stopped at the door, looked at her and said,

"That may be true. But who in the hell wants a housewife?"

Then we left: Cleopatra, Charlotte Web, Glamour, Cheyanne Foxx and myself piled in the Cady and headed to Vegas. Cheyanne whispered in Cleo's ear

"Thank you"

Cleo leaned over and kissed her on the cheek very gently. Coffee received a B on the report Cheyanne helped her with it. I never read it so I'm not sure what she put in it. Time can only tell just how expensive this experience was for Coffee.

I put in my 'Eurythmics' CD. I played 'Sweet Dreams' as we drove off headed to Vegas. What lies ahead? Your guess is as good as mines. But expect the unexpected......

THE END?

Mickey Royal resides in Los Angeles, California where he is currently writing his next book. Contact Mickey Royal personally at;

Mickey Royal
6709 La Tijera Blvd #567
LA, CA 90045

Mickeyroyal1972@gmail.com
Facebook (Mickey Royal)
mickeyroyal.com

Order Form (free shipping)

Item#   **Description**

#406   **The Pimp Game:**
              Instructional Guide.........................14.95
               by Mickey Royal

The former Hollywood king reveals secret techniques with proven results on mastering the art of submission. A look inside the mind of the master as well as a chilling peek into the shadow world. A modern-day guide parallel to The Prince by Machiavelli.

#407   **Along For The Ride......................14.95**
               by Mickey Royal

An autobiographical account of how Mickey Royal establishes The Royal Family; an organized stable of prostitutes, which runs with the efficiency of a Fortune 500 company. At the same time, this powerful family takes on crooked cops, overzealous music executives, drug lords and the Muslim Mafia to solve a six-year-old murder mystery.

#408   **Pimping Ain't Easy:**
               But Somebody's Gotta Do It...................14.95
               by Mickey Royal

Coffee, a journalism student on spring break who has been given the assignment of a lifetime. She follows Mickey Royal around for seven days as she gathers intel for her mid-term. She soon finds herself entangled in the shadow world and embarks on an adventure she won't soon forget.

Order Form (free shipping)

Item#	Description	Qty	Price
_____	_____	____	_____
_____	_____	____	_____
_____	_____	____	_____
_____	_____	____	_____

Send check or money order to:
Sharif Media
6709 La Tijera Blvd
#567
 LA, CA 90045

Or order online at: mickeyroyal.com or amazon.com
Ship To:

Name_____

Address_____

City, _____

State, Zip code_____

Phone_____

E-mail_____

Order Form (free shipping)

Item#   Description

#406   The Pimp Game:
        Instructional Guide.........................14.95
        by Mickey Royal

The former Hollywood king reveals secret techniques with proven results on mastering the art of submission. A look inside the mind of the master as well as a chilling peek into the shadow world. A modern-day guide parallel to The Prince by Machiavelli.

#407   Along For The Ride....................14.95
        by Mickey Royal

An autobiographical account of how Mickey Royal establishes The Royal Family; an organized stable of prostitutes, which runs with the efficiency of a Fortune 500 company. At the same time, this powerful family takes on crooked cops, overzealous music executives, drug lords and the Muslim Mafia to solve a six-year-old murder mystery.

#408   Pimping Ain't Easy:
        But Somebody's Gotta Do It...................14.95
        by Mickey Royal

Coffee, a journalism student on spring break who has been given the assignment of a lifetime. She follows Mickey Royal around for seven days as she gathers intel for her mid-term. She soon finds herself entangled in the shadow world and embarks on an adventure she won't soon forget.

Order Form (free shipping)

Item#	Description	Qty	Price
_____	_____	____	_____
_____	_____	____	_____
_____	_____	____	_____
_____	_____	____	_____

Send check or money order to:
Sharif Media
6709 La Tijera Blvd
#567
 LA, CA 90045

Or order online at: mickeyroyal.com or amazon.com
Ship To:

Name_____

Address_____

City, _____

State, Zip code_____

Phone_____

E-mail_____

Mickey Royal

Made in the
USA
Middletown, DE